Journeys in the Light

## The author

Jan Arriens was born in England in 1943 to Dutch parents, and grew up in New Zealand and Australia. He spent ten years as a diplomat in the Australian foreign service, and has worked as a freelance translator since 1978.

In 1987 he founded the death row correspondence organisation LifeLines after seeing a BBC TV documentary, and in that year he also became a Quaker. He is a member of Cambridge Hartington Grove meeting.

He delivered the Henry Cadbury Memorial Lecture at Friends General Conference Gathering in Hamilton, Ontario, in 1996. His other books are *The Knight and the Candle Flame* (2000), a retelling of an ancient legend, and *Seeking the Source* (2005), a collection of stories set in a mythical Indian town.

# Journeys in the Light

## Quaker stories by Jan Arriens

### Illustrations by Margaret Mence Baker

Pronoun Press

Pronoun Press is an imprint of Peter Daniels Publisher Services
35 Benthal Road, London N16 7AR, UK

"A Friend to Slaves" has replaced the previous title for this story
(Revised November 2007)

ISBN 978-0-9556183-1-4

# Contents

Foreword . . . . . . . . . . . . . . . . . . . . . .7
by Steve Whiting

Introduction . . . . . . . . . . . . . . . . . . .9
by Jan Arriens

Let Your Lives Speak . . . . . . . . . . . . .11
George Fox at Firbank Fell, 1652

A Frail Vessel . . . . . . . . . . . . . . . . .20
The voyage of the *Woodhouse*, 1657

The Coin . . . . . . . . . . . . . . . . . . . . .32
Bedfordshire, 1750

A Troublesome Friend . . . . . . . . . . . . 38
Pennsylvania, 1758

The Man in White . . . . . . . . . . . . . .44
John Woolman, America, 1763

The Lone Preacher . . . . . . . . . . . . . .53
Stephen Grellet, 1807

The Woman in Grey . . . . . . . . . . . . .59
Elizabeth Fry, 1815

A Friend to Slaves . . . . . . . . . . . . . .69
Thomas Clarkson's work, 1780 to 1846

The Fugitive . . . . . . . . . . . . . . . . . .80
Ohio, 1850

The Sheepdog . . . . . . . . . . . . . . . . .86
Wales, 1880

A Black Bible and a White Carnation  . .91
  Birmingham to Bournville, 1879 to 1900

The Enemy Within  . . . . . . . . . . . . .104
  Bermondsey, London, 1915

The Charge  . . . . . . . . . . . . . . . . .110
  England, Flanders and France, 1914 to 1919

The Two Suns  . . . . . . . . . . . . . . .119
  Bethnal Green, London, 1928

Facing the Tribunal . . . . . . . . . . . . .124
  Gold Coast (Ghana). 1939

The Choice  . . . . . . . . . . . . . . . . .128
  Netherlands, 1942

The Extra Mile  . . . . . . . . . . . . . . .136
  Italy, 1946

The Roll-Call . . . . . . . . . . . . . . . .142
  Ireland, 1947

The Dress Suit . . . . . . . . . . . . . . .145
  Amsterdam, Philadelphia and Oslo, 1947

A Brush with the Law . . . . . . . . . . . .151
  Northern France, 1960

The Outsider  . . . . . . . . . . . . . . . .156
  Faslane, Scotland, 1992

Silent Friendship  . . . . . . . . . . . . .162
  England and United States, 1994

The Opinion Poll  . . . . . . . . . . . . . .167
  England, 2006

Drawing the Threads Together  . . . . . .173
  Cambridge, 1995

# Foreword

"I keep getting ideas for children's stories" said Jan. It was October 2002 and we were on our way to buy food for a residential meeting of a dozen Quakers deep in the countryside. The meeting was of the Testimonies Committee of Quaker Peace & Social Witness (QPSW). This was a special committee. It had been asked to do "deep and wide thinking" on Quaker testimony, which is about the dynamic relationship between faith and action – "what God wants us to be and do". The meetings were short on business and long on religious and spiritual exploration, with a healthy dash of fun and good simple food thrown in. In a Quaker phrase, the members of the Committee came to know one another "in the things which are eternal".

Jan was convinced that these stories were a product of his rich experiences with Testimonies Committee. "They just keep coming to me," he said, "all I do is write them down." The result was *Seeking the Source* (2005), a collection of stories based in India, which includes wonderfully expressive illustrations from Margaret Baker.

Still stories kept coming to him. And these ones were different, more specifically about aspects of Quaker testimony. They retell well-known events in Quaker history, but there are contemporary ones here too. Many of the characters are regarded as "Quaker saints", people that embody the best of what Quakers believe they are led to be: courageous, just, and faithful to what they experience as God's purpose for them. All helped to bring a positive change in their world.

But the trouble with saints is they are distant figures. Even the ones still alive we can't always relate to. We find ourselves in awe of them. We can aspire but we can never really be like them. They are figures that we have placed on a pedestal, out of reach.

And this is what I love about these new stories of Jan's. He brings these people down from the pedestal, dusts them off and breathes life into them. He uses a key moment or episode in their lives to reveal their real human doubts, dilemmas, or moments of clarity. How did they get that insight? Where did their strength come from? Why did they keep going? He connects them to us and helps us realise that these are people with failings and frailties as well as strengths and certainties – just like us. He gives us a sense that they have played a part in something much bigger than themselves, that they have been given choices – just like us. They did not always know the outcome of their actions; what is important is that they lived faithfully. These stories encourage us to believe that we, too, can follow our deepest, truest promptings. And, if opportunity calls, we too can do extraordinary things – just like them.

These are Quaker experiences from across time and place, threaded together to make a bigger Quaker picture. For me, this tapestry of stories reveals in a quite direct way the essence of Quakerism. Next time someone asks me "Who are the Quakers?" or "What do Quakers believe?" I think I'll just give them this book.

Jan sees this as his final contribution to the work of Testimonies Committee, which was coming to an end. So ends this project, so ends the work of the committee. Or does it? I suspect that, like Margaretta in "Drawing the Threads Together", Jan and the Committee may "feel a bit lost now that it is all done". But look what happened next!

Steve Whiting
Secretary, Testimonies Committee
Quaker Peace & Social Witness

# Introduction

These stories were completed at Drawell or Draw-Well Cottage, where George Fox spent the night before preaching at Firbank Fell in June 1652: the beginning of Quakerism. The cottage has been modernised, but the old stone barn attached to the house is largely unchanged, and it is not hard to imagine Fox donning his broad brimmed Quaker hat and striding off down to the River Lune and climbing the hills on the other side to reach the fell.

A plaque beneath the great rock on which Fox preached his sermon starts with his words: "Let your lives speak". These stories seek to convey Quakerism through the lives of Friends past and present. They are intended for young and old, and for both newcomers and Friends of longer standing. They are arranged historically, but can be read in any order.

Stories are an important way of handing down tradition, and each generation needs to do so in its own way. Some stories are old, while others are new, some are historical and others made up. While, inevitably, there will be gaps, the stories are designed to build up a composite picture of Quakerism, much as one grasps the beauty of a jewel by looking at the various facets.

The stories spring from a number of sources. One has been the six years I have spent on the Testimonies Committee from 2001 until 2007. During this time we have reflected deeply on the Testimonies, and especially the fact that they have never been written down but are known for the way in which they have been lived out. A large part of my purpose in this writing has therefore been to explore the themes of peace, simplicity, truth and equality in story form. I am grateful for the support the Committee have given me, and especially for their decision to adopt the stories as part of their work. Steve Whiting, in particular, has been a constant source of encouragement.

One of the stories – "The Outsider" – concerns a member of the committee, Helen Steven, and her protests at the Faslane naval base. Other stories are also based on real Friends, in this case from my own Quaker meeting. Ruth Bell was a schoolteacher in a poor part of London in the 1920s. She would often tell the story of the boy in her class who was drawing God and how she asked how he knew what God looked like – a story of which I have now heard a number of variants, set in different places. Whether what is now almost a universal legend sprang from her experience I don't know, but her account is certainly the earliest such tale I have heard. John Brigham was appointed headmaster of the Quaker school in Waterford at the age of 29. Both were great beacons of light in my meeting. Still alive are Thurstan Shaw ("The Tribunal"), now 93, an eminent archaeologist who first came into contact with Quakerism when he took a stand as a conscientious objector in the present-day Ghana at the start of the Second World War. Margaretta Playfair, aged 94, is the "heroine" of the final story in the book. Not a member of my meeting but a good friend was John Hemming ("Silent Friendship"), the remarkable Quaker poet whose verse came to him unbidden in the night. "The Extra Mile" is based on the experience of Stephen Cary, an American Friend.

It was their lives and their example, together with the inspiration of grappling with the Testimonies, that were behind this book. I have also received a great deal of support from other people within my meeting. Elisabeth Calvert, who first introduced me to Quakerism 20 years ago, has been a steadfast support and highly discerning critic.

As in the case of *Seeking the Source*, it has been a joy to work with Margaret Baker, who has such a gift for capturing the essence of the stories in her illustrations. Finally, Peter Daniels has been a superb editor, who has not been afraid to say when something didn't work.

So in all these ways I see these stories very much as a collective process. Writing them has often felt like standing up in a Quaker meeting, drawing for one's words on the unspoken and unseen mystery that embraces us all.

Jan Arriens

# Let Your Lives Speak

Thomas Scales:

Word had come to High Haygarth from Colonel Benson's other farm near Sedbergh that a mighty preacher would be speaking at Firbank Fell the next Sunday. We should all go if we could, the steward said. It was so busy at High Haygarth that I had been unable to go to the hiring fair in Sedbergh on the Wednesday; not that I was in want of being hired, for I held a good if hard position, but there was all the excitement of the fair and the chance to meet old friends and make new ones, while it would also have been difficult to keep me separated from some of the good ale on sale; and there was also a young woman from Ingmire Hall I had hoped to see. But alas, the busyness of our work had not permitted me to go.

"We have heard this man preach," the steward said later in the week, "both on Whitsunday at Borrets Farm and on Whitsonwedonsday in the churchyard in Sedbergh. Many were convinced."

"Convinced?"

"Aye, convinced. Convinced that here before us the truth was laid forth."

"And his name, sir?" I inquired.

"Why, Fox, George Fox, a young man, not yet thirty years of age, from Leicestershire. A man of most singular temper. Thou shouldst go, Thomas, on the Sunday to hear him at Firbank."

The way to Firbank from High Haygarth ran through Sedbergh, taking the main road, but this meant a great loop and, the day dawning fair, I determined to take the direct route across the Howgills. But while shorter, it was I knew also demanding, with steep climbs and abrupt descents, and often rough underfoot. I set off early in the morning with the sun still cool on my shoulder, and made my way up to Cautley Spout. A grand climb! But hard, and I was glad that youth was on my side. Beside me, the waterfall cascaded and skipped its way down to Cautley Beck. By contrast, the spring in my stride gave way to a weary plod long afore I reached the top. Once atop the ridge I could look back down to High Haygarth, so small it could barely be descried. Turning around, there were the Howgills in all their glory rolling away to the west and the vale of the River Lune. Facing me on the other side of the valley was Firbank Fell, and beyond that again Westmorland. Who was this George Fox, I could not help wondering? Why, striding over this magnificent country, should it matter to me that I should hearken to the words of this man, as my master would have me do? What words of man could match the majesty of these mysterious, timeless hills?

But I made my way across to the nearby peak known as Calders. Here I tarried a while at the highest point, the world at my feet, with company none save for one or two more venturesome sheep. From Calders I was able to break into an easy downhill trot all the way round the great hill of Winder, Sedbergh nestling comfortably below, and on towards the river glinting in the distance between the trees.

Coming off Winder I could not but help notice that all the world seemed to be abroad that Sunday morn! On every lane there were people, some proceeding singly and others in twos and threes or little knots, all, I surmised, on their way to Firbank Fell. Reaching Howgill Lane I fell in with another young man, who returned my greeting pleasantly, revealing that he was named Robert Nicholson.

## Robert Nicholson:

"And what brings you here, Robert Nicholson?" said the youth, who had evidently come off the fells, his clothes all dusty.

"Why, I am right glad to meet you," I said, "for I am not of these parts but seek a place called Firbank Fell."

"I thought as much," said my newfound companion. "For that is where I too am bound and, if I am not mistaken, so too are all those out and about this fine morning. Is it this George Fox that you are going to hear?"

"I am indeed," I replied, "but not for the first time, for I am already acquainted with the power of his speech."

"You have already heard him speak?" Thomas Scales asked me eagerly. "I have walked a fair hour, up the steep fells and down again, for a man whom I know but by reputation, and that most slenderly."

I paused. "You shall not be disappointed," I said solemnly. "I heard him this last Wednesday, at the Sedbergh hiring fair."

"You were seeking work?"

"Yes, I have come from Preston Patrick in search of employment. But what I have found is far beyond any mortal service that might come my way. My ears and eyes have been opened. Never have I heard such a man."

"Tell me more, Robert."

"Why, it was as the hiring fair was drawing to a close. Many young people had come to be hired. I found a good position, starting soon, and was well pleased with my good fortune. I wandered through the little town, a tune upon my lips, when rounding the corner I came upon the churchyard. There, perched in a yew tree, and preaching like one possessed, was a man whose very gaze at fifty yards did stop me in my tracks."

"What did he say?"

"He spoke of the everlasting Truth. He spoke of how Christ Jesus had spoken to us, the ordinary people, and not only to priests and teachers, and that he, Christ Jesus, was the way to God. What those words meant I could not truly tell, but I knew they were true, and they pierced me like an arrow. There were teachers and priests there, among those listening, but none durst speak against him, until at last a captain asked him if he would not go into the church, as a fit place for him to preach in. But this man, George Fox, was raised into a temper, and spoke of the wickedness of steeplehouses, as he called them, and of those falsely paid to preach in them. The truth, he declared, was within ourselves and not bound up with any man in fine vestments or any building made by man. One man standing by, evidently himself a preacher, declared, 'This man speaks with authority,' and so he did. I heard but the last few moments of his discourse, and now would hear him without restriction."

Thomas Scales seemed much startled at my words, and fell silent. Just as we were about to cross the little bridge below Bramaskew farm, we stepped aside for a young woman coming along the river bank. As though wrenched from the reflection into which my words had plunged him, Thomas came suddenly alive, and greeted Alice Parke.

## Alice Parke:

Thomas asked me if I, too, were bound for the church on Firbank Fell, and introduced his fresh acquaintance Robert Nicholson, who inquired if I had come from far.

"Why no," I replied, "I have come from Ingmire Hall, not a mile from here." And I explained that the Otways, for whom I worked, had heard from one of their tenants of a man of most uncommon power preaching in the hamlet of Brigflatts and that we should not miss the chance to hear him speak. I did not much care for lengthy sermons, but it was a fine Sunday morning. Thomas Scales was, I thought, a handsome young man, and it was but my regret that High Haygarth, Colonel Benson's other farm (for he owned Borrets, at Brigflatts), was not nearer Sedbergh.

I soon found that Robert Nicholson paid me more than passing attention. I was glowing like the buttercups in the fields, when, ascending into the woods, we came upon John Blaykling.

## John Blaykling:

Ah! I confess I did linger on the path and that my heart beat faster when Alice Parke and her companions caught me up. A finer young woman was not to be found within twenty miles. Much was their astonishment when I told them that George Fox had been staying with our family at Draw-Well Cottage by Bramaskew. Four nights he spent with us, and never had I been in the presence of such a man. We had with us at one point one Captain Henry Ward from Grayrigg, aged 65, a man of fine moral temper and much determination. Rarely have I seen a man so discomposed. He had heard Fox speak inside the churchyard and, after spending time in discourse with him at the cottage, drew me aside and said that Fox's "very eyes pierced him through" – as indeed they did me.

But I explained to my new companions that we were also troubled. George Fox and my father Thomas had set off for Firbank Fell earlier in the morning. My father was much concerned, for Fox was to speak after two other, local men: Francis Howgill and John Audland. Both were Seekers, as they called them, and not far from Fox in their views, but they were both lay-preachers, receiving some payment.

"Oh," exclaimed Robert Nicholson, "I heard him denounce 'hireling priests' in Sedbergh churchyard, and could not but help think that I myself was a hireling, seeking work at the hiring fair. Is not the labourer worthy of his hire?"

"It is a fair point," I said. "I know both Francis and John as good and true men, and that they take some payment is of no import. But the paid priesthood drives Fox to a frenzy. To him it means the old established Church, whether Roman or of England; to him it smacks of authority and hypocrisy."

"So what will Fox do," asked Alice Parke, "when Howgill and Audland preach?"

"That we will find out," I replied. "For all his power, George Fox is also a fiery man, and he may denounce them."

So it was that the four of us climbed the eastern side of Firbank Fell, coming out onto the lane on the other side. From there it was but a few minutes walk to the small church that was our destination. But the lane was thronged with people, and it was only by striking out into the fields and passing behind the great mass of rock that we were able to reach the back of the church. It was full. People were craning in through the windows, while others – many hundreds, it seemed – were simply sitting outside on the grass.

## Thomas Scales:

"There he is!" whispered John, pointing to a man nearby. George Fox was standing just outside the church window, gazing at the earth and listening earnestly, glancing up just once or twice. His was a severe look, and his hands and fingers were forever moving, and tapping upon his breast.

He appeared to catch the eye of a man within the church, who looked much agitated. John and some others went up to Fox. I heard them say

in a low voice that Howgill and Audland were both good men, and that
he, Fox, should not be hard on them. He replied in a bold voice that he
could not be sure what he would do, for he would wait on the leadings of
the Lord. Francis Howgill – for it was he who had been inside – now
emerged. With a strange look in his eye, he declared that Fox might
have "killed him with a crab apple", such was the power of the look that
Fox shot him. Great was the tension as we waited on Fox to respond.
After what seemed like time without end, Fox made no reply but left
them to stride off up the fellside behind the church. I saw him stoop to
gather water from a brook in his hands.

Some moments later Fox appeared on top of the great rock a short
distance from the church. It was early afternoon. He stood there in his
broad brimmed hat, legs slightly apart. Such was his authority that as
we stood there, silently, a hush suddenly fell upon us all. People stood
up and crowded together in the hollow in front of the natural stone pul-
pit. There were hundreds of people there – perhaps even a thousand.
Some spilled over onto the steep slopes around the rock, and some even
stood behind it.

## Alice Parke:

After the crowd of people had settled down and were standing there attentively he kept us in silence for, oh, I don't know how long, but it was certainly quite a while. At first a tremor ran through the crowd. How long would he keep us waiting in silence? Would he say something about the lay preachers and how it was that they were being paid? We looked at him, but amidst the silent power and tension that was so clear just from the way he was standing, there was also a calmness about him. Much to my surprise, I found this spreading over me and, I later discovered, so did everyone there. I found myself no longer wondering when he was going to speak or what he might say. Instead, I felt gathered up in what I felt to be a great ocean of peacefulness.

And then he spoke, at first gently and then more and more strongly. He gestured to the church nearby and asked whether it and the ground it stood on were more holy than where we were all standing. So Jesus had also been in a temple but said, "Learn of me," and we – yes, we ordinary people – should learn from what we all knew *within*.

## Thomas Scales:

"What canst thou say?" The words rang in my ears so that for minutes I no longer heard what he was saying. It was not priests and it was not books, it was not churches and not fine services, but what we ourselves could say. How could I, a mere young farmhand, have anything to say? But he bade us let our lives speak, and let our light shine, so that our works might be seen.

Oh, my friends, what openings had I on that day! The truth was at hand, and it lay within – the everlasting truth, the everlasting gospel, I heard him say in a voice that now seemed far away. Once I was able to listen properly again, I found that he was talking about how the priests had taken the Scriptures but not in the same spirit in which they were given forth. Temples we made with our own hands, but we should know that we were the temples of God. He spoke wonderfully of many parables, and it was as though Jesus himself were telling them to the multitude who had gathered on the mountain and were sharing their fishes and loaves. Quite what it was that we were sharing, with George Fox and among ourselves, I could not be sure, but I knew it was a mystery that was deep and true, and that the light of which he spoke would never leave me.

## Robert Nicholson:

I had already heard George Fox at the Sedbergh fair, but hearing him again on Firbank Fell stirred me no less. He spoke with an awesome power and a certainty that swept over us all. Here was a man who knew his Bible through and through, but who also lived the words on those dead pages; a man who took us to places where we had never been or even glimpsed before, who gave us hope and made the world a place full of the Light and the Spirit. Our world is such a troubled one, with people believing and saying such different things, that I have been at a loss where to turn. Now, at last, have I glimpsed the truth.

Full three hours he spoke, pausing only one or two times to take a draught of water, when we, too, would hastily take some refreshment and move our limbs for a moment or two. And then he would be off again, often as though reading our thoughts. Even the children fell quiet, and I am not sure that so much as a single person left before Fox was done.

When he did at last end, exhorting us to live in the spirit of Truth that was available to us all, we continued to stand for some minutes, motionless. Then, silently, we all went our separate ways: some north up the road to Tebay, others down the hillside and into the villages of Westmorland, and many of us retracing our steps over the fell, through the wood and down to the river.

## Alice Parke:

Three hours! How was it possible that I could have listened for so long without restlessness!

We came to the bridge where our ways parted. Our hearts were full and we knew that our lives would never quite be the same again. I took my leave gravely from the three young men, and we agreed that we should gather at the meeting for worship that was to be held at one of the farms in Brigflatts. I saw those young men anew from when we first met near the gate, knowing that they too, like me, had been taken to a wordless place, and that we were children of the Light.

## John Blaykling:

Draw-Well Cottage was not far off and it was here that I left my companions. I would fain have offered them something to eat, but explained that I was just returning to fetch some clothes. George Fox was to walk that night to Crosslands, some ten miles to the south, to stay with John Audland. I wished to go too, to spend one more day in the power of this man before he strode off to other parts.

Never have I seen Alice Parke look so beautiful, but it was a radiance from both within and beyond herself, and I knew that she and I and Tom and Robert had all been touched by that same force.

## Robert Nicholson:

Thomas and I walked together some distance, talking as I had never conversed with any other mortal before. What worlds were opened up before us! To tarry the longer with him I accompanied him to the top of Winder, from where he showed me a path by which I might reach Sedbergh comfortably in not much time.

We parted wordlessly, knowing that what was not said meant more than aught we could put into words. I watched him stride off towards Calders, as though there were no upward slope beneath his feet.

## Thomas Scales:

It was hard taking leave of Robert, although we agreed to meet again soon. How good it had been to share with him, and the others. I knew too that I would be seeing Alice again, but that what mattered was something far greater than the idle thoughts I entertained for her on the bridge that morning.

Now, once more, I walked on the high fells, this time with the sun setting, glinting on the distant sea. Again, I was swept up in the timeless majesty of those grand mountains, where just that morning I had been all alone and yet so close to all around me that I had wondered what more a mortal being might ever have to add.

Now I knew.

# A Frail Vessel

The *Woodhouse* was not a big ship. It was not designed to take eleven passengers and crew of five. It was certainly not designed to make an Atlantic crossing. And yet, here it was, slamming into a strong westerly breeze that was building up into a gale. The small craft rose and sank on the high, rolling waves.

The master, Robert Fowler, had forbidden the passengers to come on deck as the storm gathered. He could not have non-seafarers slithering and crashing about on deck. As it was, his crew needed to be certain they were fastened at all times to the lifelines he had made sure were in place. He could not afford to lose so much as one of his precious crew overboard and was thankful that he did not have a large, square-rigged ship on which the crew had to go aloft and could so easily lose their lives.

The storm grew in intensity. For eighteen hours in succession the master did not go below. When the storm was at its height he had all sail taken in except for a tiny triangle, set in such a way as to keep the vessel pointing into the wind at all times.

The wind reached a peak. The foam was blown horizontally off the cresting waves. For a few minutes, everything turned white. The *Woodhouse* rose and fell gallantly, but the fear was that she would be knocked side-on to the waves, to wallow helplessly like a stricken bird.

"Thou hast her not for nothing. She is needed for the service of Truth." Once again the mysterious words came to the master. This time the situation was too perilous for him to wonder whether he was imagining things and he simply drew strength and comfort from them.

He first heard the words when building the ship. Robert Fowler was a successful master mariner from Bridlington in Yorkshire. He had long wanted to build a boat with graceful lines, but one that could also carry a goodly cargo. It was not a boat with which to venture far afield but would serve his purpose admirably of carrying cargoes in the coastal trade from Yorkshire. Perhaps, at most, he might venture to Holland if there were no more wars with the Low Countries.

He had wrestled long and hard with the words. How could he be sure that they did not spring from his imagination? All sorts of people went about claiming to have heard extraordinary things. There were those who believed fervently that the Second Coming of Jesus was near. Why, not long before he had heard a man preaching that the execution of King Charles just eight years before was a sign that the New Kingdom of God was at hand. There was to be a fifth monarchy as foreseen by King Nebuchadnezzar in a dream.

There were all sort of other sects too, some that made more sense to him, like the Quakers. Five years ago in 1652 he had heard one of them, William Dewsbury, preach about the power of the light within us all. His words pierced him to the core. If we were but quiet within ourselves and listened closely enough, we would find guidance: "Wait in the Light, that the Word of the Lord may dwell plentifully in you." It was not just the message that touched him but also the quiet authority and deep kindness of this man, who had been through so much. The truth lay on William Dewsbury like a cloak.

The words were not to be disregarded, mysterious though they were. What could it mean, that the vessel built by his own loving hands was "not for nothing" but for the "service of Truth"? Robert Fowler turned to others in the Quaker meeting to which he belonged. They sat silently in a circle for two and a half hours, just one man or woman occasionally saying a few words. "Thou must follow the leading, Robert," they concluded. For reasons he could not understand, the thought of New England, in the colony of America, kept entering his mind.

One night he had a vivid and powerful dream. In it he took his vessel to London. When he awoke the next morning the dream stayed with him so strongly that he felt it must be a message. But then again, it was just a dream. He wrestled with the memory, as it did not make sense to sail his ship to London. It had taken him so long to build, and he had lavished such care on the project, that it went against the grain to go on such a madcap errand; aye, against the grain, in just the same way that he had always worked *with* the grain as he carefully prepared the timbers for his vessel.

Nevertheless, much against his will, Master Mariner Robert Fowler sailed the *Woodhouse* on its maiden voyage down the east coast of England and then up the River Thames to London. It handled beautifully and he felt a deep sense of satisfaction at having built such a fine, seaworthy boat. Arriving at London docks he could see other seasoned seamen casting admiring glances at the *Woodhouse* as the vessel glided gracefully through the water to its mooring.

After he had tied up in the docks Robert Fowler sought out Friends, taking with him a letter of introduction from his Quaker meeting. Before long he discovered that a group of eleven Quakers were looking for a ship to take them to America. Try as they might they had been unable to find one since the masters of vessels could be severely punished in the colonies for carrying Quaker passengers. The Friends he met in London were convinced that Fowler's arrival was the work of the Lord and "that it must be so".

This, Robert Fowler knew deep down, was the leading the Friends in Bridlington had spoken about, but still he resisted it. The eleven friends – seven men and four women, five of whom had been to the New England colonies before – were full of enthusiasm. Robert Fowler was full of gloom. His boat was far too small for so many people. It was not built for an Atlantic crossing. There would be Dutch warships to worry about in the English Channel, and the risk of hurricanes later in the summer as they approached America. And how he was longing to make use of the *Woodhouse* for the coastal trade. There were good cargoes of hides in Yorkshire waiting to be shipped!

Now these wretched people brimming with eagerness were swarming all over his ship as though they owned it. Guidance was all very well, but needed to be tempered by common sense and discernment. His irritation mounted and he caught himself wondering just what sort of a mariner God could be. He had known men of great faith who never returned from ocean voyages. As it was, it felt like the loss of his life: he would be parted from his wife and children, and from all the everyday things he enjoyed. He was a man who loved life, and now he would as willingly have died as have gone on the voyage.

It was just at this point that a small band of men led by a naval officer made their way up the ship's gangplank. The master of the *Woodhouse* knew straight away who they were: a press-gang.

"I seek able-bodied men for the service of our Lord Protector Cromwell in the English Navy!" stated their leader.

"And I need my men in the service of the truth, to take these good people to the colonies," replied Robert Fowler evenly. "I cannot spare them."

"Quakers!" The naval officer all but spat out the word. "The more fool you if you would take them across the waters. If by some miracle your poor vessel were to make it to the other side, you would be clapped in irons by the authorities. I shall take the men I need."

And without further ado the officer had the full crew of the *Woodhouse* lined up and selected the men he needed. Fowler was left with just two men and three boys.

Maybe God was coming to his senses. "Friends," he said to the assembled company, "you see, I now lack the necessary crew to take ye across. I beseech ye, consider again whether you might not be mistaken in this endeavour."

It was just two days later that he received another visitor on board: George Fox. Standing on the poop of the *Woodhouse* by the wheel, the leader of the new Quaker movement preached a mighty sermon, about an ocean of light and an ocean of darkness. Seamen on the quayside stopped and listened. A great light, Fox said, would travel with this ship: the same light that each and every one there had within them and which would unfailingly guide them and give them strength if they would but heed it. Robert Fowler was stirred by Fox's words, but still his doubts persisted.

Stores were brought on board and hammocks slung in the hold for the eleven Friends. On the first of June 1657 they set sail, stopping briefly off the east coast of Kent, where William Dewsbury came on board to see them off. He had been in prison for several years since Robert first heard him preach, and was not released until the year before. "Listen to the inner voice," he said. "Just as thou felt the Spirit abroad in the field when we met, so also mayest thou feel the Presence on the great wide ocean. Go within, go into the deeps, even as the fish."

Robert Fowler had stood many times on the poop of a sailing ship, marvelling at the ever changing moods of the sea and the majesty of the skies and the stars, but rarely had he been out of sight of land. His ship was too small; he lacked crew; he would be at the mercy of the elements. But William Dewsbury's calm words once again touched him. "The unspoken knowledge we carry within us is like a flame. Know too that we can each kindle a fire by bringing our own sparks, but then it will be a poor fire, as we will ever be blowing at our own sparks for to raise them up, and seeing only what we ourselves can see by the light of our own small sparks. But bring together the sparks of us all as we are gathered together in worship, or in our daily dealings, and we shall have a sturdy fire, and see the more widely and fully from what each of us there is able to see by their own lights. Carry that flame across the ocean, and it will carry thee too."

The small band of Friends weighed anchor and continued on their journey. Strong southerly winds forced them to seek shelter in Portsmouth. On resuming their journey the *Woodhouse* soon fell into the company of three large English ships bound for Newfoundland. Although much smaller, the beautifully designed and speedy *Woodhouse* was able to keep up with them without difficulty. They travelled together for nearly two days. It seemed a good omen.

"It would be well to travel all the way across the ocean in their company," observed Robert Hodgson, one of the travelling Quakers, "especially if we were to meet bad weather."

"It would indeed," replied the master. "And they can give us protection if we were to meet Dutch warships, which are believed to be in the vicinity."

Robert Hodgson rejoined the others. One of their number, Humphrey Norton, was a quiet, gentle man with a faraway look in his eye.

"I have seen danger. There are those closing in on us who would take our lives," he said. "But tell the master not to fear; I have a vision that we shall be carried away as in a mist."

Robert Hodgson went back on deck to tell the master, who was with Paul Wainwright the navigator, or pilot as he was known. He was not a Friend, and not in sympathy with Friends. A lean, thin man, he was angry: with the master for undertaking such a madcap venture; with the Quakers for their foolish ways; with the cramp and confinement of the little vessel; with the wind and the waves, which always seemed against them; and most of all with himself, for agreeing to remain with the venture when the others were press-ganged, staying on only because his ill-temper made it so difficult for him to find work. His twelve-year-old son Stephen was also one of the five crew.

Paul Wainwright's black beard quivered with anger. "We are not to rely on any mist descending from a clear blue sky!" he roared. "Our safety lies with the other ships. That is the course we will follow."

"He is right," said Master Fowler reluctantly. "The chance to travel in convoy is God-given."

The others came up on deck to join Robert Hodgson. As they sat in worship, hands joined together, the cry went out from the lookout: "Sail on the east horizon!"

It was a great Dutch warship. The three larger English vessels immediately changed course, heading north. But the Friends on the deck rocked backwards and forwards, saying, "Not that way! Not that way! Steer a straight course! Mind the Lord!"

The pilot's fury knew no bounds. "Helmsman, change course and bide with the other ships! Steer north-west by north," he commanded. But the circle of Friends on the deck kept swaying to and fro. "Not that way! Not that way! Steer the straight course!"

All eyes turned to the master. What was to be his leading? Was he to follow the three vessels he had so fortunately joined, or was he to follow the visions and inner promptings of his fellow Quakers? He hesitated. Already the three vessels were drawing away. What could this little band of fervent Friends know of the might of the sea or the perils of navigation? And yet – and yet: he recalled the words of William Dewsbury, and how each with their own little light could together illumine the whole.

As he hesitated, the wind began to change, much to the disadvantage of the pursuing Dutch ship, and a mist miraculously sprang up over the waters. Both the Dutch ship and the three English vessels were lost to sight. "Steer the straight course!" the Quakers continued to cry, swaying forward as they did so. "See the Lord leading our vessel, even as it were a man leading a horse by the head!"

The *Woodhouse* made its escape. For several days they met fair winds. Then the wind built in intensity, until the Friends were no longer able to meet on deck in the open. From the forecastle came their cries as they called out instructions to the pilot. "Bear starboard, bear starboard, and thou shalt escape the worst winds."

The pilot, with the Master's agreement, refused, as the seas were too high to risk sailing side-on to the wind. It was then that everything turned white, with sheets of rain, horizontal spray and huge foaming seas. Despite the terrific strains the boat handled beautifully, with the wheel lashed down and one tiny sail hauled over to windward; the sail made the boat try to go one way and the rudder the other, so that the boat kept its head into the wind. But this was the eye of the storm, and Master Fowler could not help reflecting on how it could have been avoided, if he had heeded what the Friends were directing him to do.

The storm blew itself out. After a day or two of good progress the winds died away altogether. Now for three days the *Woodhouse* was becalmed. Down below, however, it was anything but still and calm. For all the lack of wind there was still a swell: tiny, but enough for the boat to rock backwards and forwards. It would lurch this way and that, building up a frightening momentum that sent everything inside crashing and cascading one way and then the other. The water in the half-empty wooden watertanks crashed and banged like drunken elephants. Floorboards creaked in agony. Such was the noise that on the third morning Robert Fowler awoke thinking that the ship must be moving along briskly, only to go up on deck and find that the *Woodhouse* was still wallowing aimlessly.

The Friends came up on deck. The pilot looked like thunder. They sat in their wailing circle. "Steer left!" came the sound of Mary Weatherhead's and Dorothy Waugh's voices high above the rest.

"There is no wind, can't you see, you simpletons!" snarled the pilot. The Friends looked up. The pilot's face was like a contorted mask. "I have half a mind to lash some sense into you."

"Friend," said the master, "I will not have such talk on my vessel.

They have been right before, and perhaps we should listen to them."

But the truth was that the master himself was far from convinced by the promptings of the little band. So often the course they wanted to steer defied any logic, and he would feel obliged to ignore what they said.

So again it proved this time. Not long after the group on deck had clapped hands and urged the master to bear to port, a breeze stirred and the *Woodhouse* began to move through the water again. The master, however, continued to head west; why ever should they turn south?

The wind kept strengthening and the next day built up into the second storm. It was not as severe as the first, but the *Woodhouse* did take two giant waves in quick succession. They loomed up suddenly and, standing on the poop near the wheel, Robert Fowler watched as the great mass of ghastly green water came crashing down amidships. Down below, the Friends watched as water forced its way through the hatches.

The master was growing anxious. The storms and the days without wind meant that they were making little progress. Their stores were being depleted and water supplies were running low. He could not help noticing that the more anxious he grew and the less notice he took of the clapping and swaying of the Friends, the slower and more difficult their progress. He tried to recall Fox's and Dewsbury's words about following the light and trusting one's leadings, but he could not simply disregard the knowledge and experience that made him a master mariner. It made it difficult for him to join the other Friends in worship, as he would then find himself caught up in their attempts to discern the course they should steer. Even the pilot's son Stephen appeared to regard him with barely disguised contempt.

"Sail ho!" came the cry from a sailor high up the mast. Putting his telescope to his eye Robert Fowler made out a large vessel that appeared to be a warship. It was a signalling that the *Woodhouse* should draw near; but might it be an enemy frigate?

It was a time for instant decision. Robert Fowler had so often been wrong following his own reasoning and experience. It was as though when he doubted, the sea rose up against them. Now he did what he could to make out his inner voice. The life of all those on board was in his hands. This time he did not hold back but opened himself up entirely. With a sense of certainty, he received an unspoken message that all was well, that he could trust, and that he should speak with the great vessel.

The ship turned out to be an English merchantman on its way back to London. The two ships stopped in mid sea and the crew and travelling Friends on the *Woodhouse* were able to send back messages to their loved ones. The merchantman also provided the *Woodhouse* with some much-needed supplies.

Robert Fowler took stock. They had been at sea for five weeks and had covered not even one thousand miles. They were no more than one third of the way. He could trust, and he *would* trust; but they would still need every good fortune to accomplish their mission. They had run into a third storm. The hurricane season would soon be upon them. The seriously exhausted and sullen crew with their dark forebodings and the Quaker passengers with their apparently insane optimism were like the ocean of darkness and ocean of light of which George Fox spoke. Robert Fowler was not sure that he could hold the tensions.

It was then that Humphrey Norton sought him out by the mainmast. "Friend," he said softly, out of earshot of the baleful pilot, "fear not, for I have been in strange communion. The answer I have received is comfortable; all shall be well. What I see without seeing is that we shall make safe landfall at the end of the next month."

Despite the objections of the pilot, Fowler kept the *Woodhouse* on the more southerly course on which his passengers kept insisting. His whole bearing assumed a new assurance that infected even the remaining crew, including the pilot's son. Each morning as the vessel sped through the water in sparkling seas the master would call the three young members of the crew to the mainmast or to his cabin and give them instruction. They learned the use of the navigation instrument known as the astrolabe, how to place the pegs in the traverse board to plot the vessel's progress and how to find the latitude by measuring the altitude of the North Star with the cross-staff.

"What about boxing the compass?" said the master. "Can you do that?" The boys laughed. In unison they recited all thirty-two points of the compass as they had been taught: "North, north-by-east, nor-nor-east, north-east by north, north-east, north-east by east, east north-east, east by north, east, east by south…"

"And now let's see who is fastest," said the master. Off the boys went, at breakneck speed. Always, Stephen Wainwright was first. The Friends standing by would smile and try to repeat the thirty-two points of the compass for themselves.

With fair winds the last two thirds of the crossing – nearly two thousand miles – were completed in just three weeks. The pilot consistently wanted to steer a course more northerly than that discerned by the nodding Friends, who would now call out "west-south-west!" or "south-west by west!" But the master was clear that their course should follow the guidance the group was receiving.

For all but three days of rough weather the Friends were able to assemble on deck, which they did at the same time each day. When the Master ordered them to remain below they held their meetings in the cramped quarters known as the forecastle. This was a dank and dismal place. Water sloshed about, there were mouldering coils of rope and old sailcloth lying around, and scraps of food would often be flung into some distant cranny by the cook. It was not possible to stand up straight. The only light came in through the small hatchway, which would be shut in bad weather. For light they would then have to use a spout lamp, with a cotton wick pushed down the spout. Old fat from the cook was all they had as lamp-oil. The lamp, which hung from a hook, gave out acrid smoke and a bad smell, and but little light. Sometimes the Friends would hold their meetings in total darkness.

Now, however, the *Woodhouse* was slicing through the sunlit water, its bow rising and falling like a prancing horse. America was near. On one particular day, the Friends felt they should meet much earlier than normal. Having all along said that they should sail a more southerly course, the Friends now, in a spirit of obedience, declared that they should turn north.

At the Master's command, the *Woodhouse* changed course. The pilot continued to protest, for the northerly course could only mean running parallel with this part of the coast, and he was triumphant all the next day when no land appeared. The Friends told the master, however, that it had been opened to them that "we may look abroad in the evening". And so it was. Amid all the rejoicing at the astonishing sight of a smudge of land on the horizon after so many weeks at sea, the band of Friends joined on deck in prayer to give thanks. They felt the power of

the unseen presence among them, and the words came to them: "The seed in America shall be as the sands of the sea." The Friends wept openly, with a sense of fullness and joy.

They reached a great river where it ran into the sea. The Friends were sure that they were meant to sail up the estuary, but the pilot again resisted. Only when morning came did he realise that the Friends were right in saying he could have taken either of the two available passages, but that one was better than the other. It was then that Paul Wainwright's doubts at last crumbled.

On 31 July 1657 the *Woodhouse* reached New Amsterdam, or what is now New York. This was in Dutch hands, and as it turned out was the safest place for the Quakers to have made landfall. They were courteously received by the Governor, Pieter Stuyvesant. It remained only to proceed to Rhode Island – a place of religious liberty, where there was a small Quaker presence – for the Friends to disembark. From there they would proceed to preach tolerance in the harsh New England colonies, where a number of them would be severely punished.

Two days before reaching New Amsterdam, Robert Fowler and Robert Hodgson had each had a vision in which they saw the *Woodhouse* in great danger. When they left the Dutch settlement to sail to Rhode Island they indeed found their ship swept through the treacherous Hell's Gate, which no vessel had navigated before, threading a passage through the swift tides and the perilous rocks no more than a yard either side of the ship. All the way a school of fish followed behind.

Safely in the broad expanse of Long Island Sound, the Friends gathered on deck for what was to be their final meeting for worship. Master

Fowler joined them, as did the pilot. Robert Hodgson spoke briefly and simply at the beginning of the meeting to give thanks for their miraculous deliverance. After a long silence, the Master rose to his feet to speak. Much though they were in tune with the deep silence, some could not but help wondering what fine words the master would manage to find to mark the end of their journey.

"Friends," said Robert Fowler, "As some of ye have witnessed with your own eyes, throughout the day a school of fish have strangely pursued our vessel, close by our rudder. Wherefore I cannot say; it is not a sight I have ever seen before. What are these fish? And why have they followed our vessel so strongly? If they are an escort, why then do they swim behind the ship? They speak to me even as the deeps of the sea, yet why I cannot say."

He sat down again. For many minutes the Friends sat with his words. The sun and the gentle sea wind played on their faces. At last, Mary Clark rose. "When we embarked on our journey, George Fox bade us godspeed, telling us of the ocean of darkness and the ocean of light that we should encounter. With us on our journey, like the school of fish, have been the prayers and blessings of those we left behind.

"Our dear vessel has been led like a horse by an unseen presence: One that has ever been with us. The course we should steer has opened up before us, even as we have seen our ship led by the light.

"No ship will steer a course without a guiding hand, and so also must we chart our own course through life. We do so not alone, but led by a love unseen, knowing the while that we, too, are part of the mighty ocean."

# The Coin

Thomas Bowden was bored. It was a hot day. He quite enjoyed ploughing, walking behind the two giant horses, Castor and Pollux, but it was near the end of the day. Like the twin stars after which they were named, they were bright and needed little guidance. Thomas would find his mind wandering off or, to amuse himself, would make some fancy turns when he reached the ends of the field. He knew his master would not see or scold him, as he was working on a new barn. Besides, he was a kind and fair man, although as a farmhand Thomas did not much like having to go to the unadorned little meeting house each Sunday – or first day, as the Quakers strangely called it – and sit in silence for an hour or more.

What he did like was to be in the open. He knew the names of all of the trees and could recognise every bird call; he knew the movements of

the badgers, stoats and foxes and could read the sky like the back of his hand.

At one end of the field there stood an enormous oak tree. Here, Thomas would perform a particularly elaborate, slow turn, and sometimes even pause altogether so that the three of them could benefit from the shade. On one such occasion he drove the horses right round the tree, in a kind of stately dance, through the nettles and giant willow herb, almost venturing onto the baked clay road that lay glinting in the sun.

So bright was the light off the road that it took him a moment to realise that something also lay glinting in the earth the great beasts had just upturned. "Whoa," he exclaimed, bringing the horses to a halt. He went back to look at what had caught his eye. There, to his astonishment, lying in the broken soil was a gold half-guinea. Ten shillings and sixpence. A small fortune. It was an old coin, as it bore the rather fierce, fat face of Queen Anne, who was long since dead.

Thomas looked at it wonderingly. How could it have been lost beside such a small road? The nearest town of any size – Bedford – was twelve miles away. But a half-guinea it was. That was several months' wages. The ploughing was nearly done and, like many other agricultural labourers in the area, he had been planning to go to town for the autumn fair.

He wondered whether to tell the farmer. The Quakers, though, were so against excess and finery. Telling him would just cause complications. No; he would just quietly pocket the money. The fact that it was such an old coin meant that it would not have been lost recently. No-one was being harmed.

He finished the ploughing. The final furrows were not as straight as the other ones, but Thomas hardly noticed.

"Well done, Thomas," said his master when he returned, "for finishing that big field. Now I expect you will be wanting to go to Bedford for the fair."

Thomas flushed a bright red. He felt the coin burn a hole in his pocket. "Telling the truth", by which the Quakers set such store, was not just a matter of not telling lies: it meant being open and honest and having nothing to hide. But then he also thought of how hard he had worked all through the summer and what a wonderful time he could have in Bedford with the good fortune that had come his way. Swallowing hard, he smiled brightly and promised to be back in two days.

The next morning dawned fair and clear. There was just a hint of autumn in the air. Thomas strode off down the baked road with a spring in his stride. The sun was dancing in the leaves of the trees, there was a gentle breeze and the birds were singing but Thomas noticed none of these. In his mind's eye he saw himself seated at a bench in Bedford, an enormous tankard of ale before him. He would order a "threepenny ordinary": meat, broth and beer. He would meet up with his boyhood friends Alan and Will, they would tell stories and they would sing. Aye, how they would sing! He would stand on the table and delight the assembled gathering with his fine, rich voice. He would order beer all round; even the best beer was only a penny a quart. And then there was a serving wench, Maisie Brown, he particularly fancied. As for the food, visions of jugged hare, bubbling beef stew, grilled capons and mutton pie drifted through his mind. There would be skittles, backgammon and other games to play, and dancing in the square. He might even try some of the best claret from the vintner's – something he had never had before. And then he would treat himself to a featherbed "with necessary apparel for one man one night", all for the cost of no more than a penny.

Which inn would he go to? He rather liked the Jolly Brewer, but then there was also the Fox. He smiled. Of course. It would have to be the Fox. That led him to wonder what other names Friends might give to a public house. The Gathered Meeting? The Inward Light? The Elder and Overseer? He laughed out loud.

With so much to think about and look forward to, the journey passed quickly. He strode through the great forest and crossed the river by the rickety footbridge, not even noticing that the riverbed was almost dry. Once or twice he vaguely heard the sound of rustling in the bushes as a deer ran off, but didn't bother to look as his mind was elsewhere. He was thinking particularly about Maisie Brown, and was only jolted back into reality when he realised that a large, warm drop of rain had just landed on his nose. Glancing up he saw that huge, fluffy white clouds had built up that were just beginning to turn black. Never mind, the first houses of Bedford were already coming into sight. He would soon be seated in the Fox, tankard in hand.

Thomas patted his pocket reassuringly, as though to give the great coin encouragement for all the work it had before it. It was not there. He patted his other pocket. It was not there either. He began patting himself all over, as though being attacked by a swarm of midges. Hiding behind a tree he struggled out of his clothes, shaking out every single garment he was wearing. Standing all but naked in the glade, and despite the now quite heavy rain, he found himself bathed in a cold sweat. As he shook out his shirt the pitiful few coins his master had given him in wages, with a little extra for the festivities in Bedford, fell out of his top pocket. Scrabbling feverishly among the rest of his clothes, he discovered to his dismay that the stitching in his trousers pocket had come apart. The half-guinea was gone.

For a moment Thomas sat stunned in the glade as big, fat drops of rain continued to fall. There was only one thing to do. He would have to retrace his steps. Donning his clothes again he glanced up at the sky. The clouds were piled up magnificently but were drifting away. Hardly any rain had in fact fallen, which was just as well as he would have no hope at all of finding the coin if it turned muddy and there were puddles on the road.

As the rain cleared, songbirds set up a tremendous chorus, led by the blackbirds. That was always a good sign, he reflected. Birds only celebrated like that when they knew the rain was over.

A little way further on, he was astonished to find that he had crossed the river in the woods. He didn't remember that at all. The bridge was very unsteady and perhaps it was here that the coin had dropped out. He peered down into the water below. It was shallow and clear and there was no sign of the coin, although it was interesting to see that for all the lack of water there were still shoals of tiny fish darting about.

A little further into the forest he was startled by the sound of a deer scampering off at the sound of his approach. He wondered who was the more startled, himself or the deer. Watching keenly he could tell from the odd movement of a bush where the deer had gone, and then caught a fleeting glimpse of a white tail before the animal disappeared into a thicket. He wondered how such large animals managed to hide themselves so well in the woods. Where did they sleep, and why were they so hard to find when you were looking for them?

As he looked for the coin and kept an eye out for the weather, he noticed how the leaves on the chestnuts were turning brown and how difficult it was to tell whether this was because they were turning colour as autumn came on or because it had been so dry. Looking up anxiously at the clouds he noticed the black rooks circling in the air and, as he emerged from the forest, spotted a kite hovering. How possibly could they see something as small as a vole or field mouse from such a height? How could they maintain their position in the air so exactly?

It was a long time since he had eaten. He came to a hedge with some blackberry bushes, but the fruit was small, dry and hard. The hawthorn berries, too, were shrivelled up and he wondered how the birds would cope through the winter.

Thomas came to a stream and was so thirsty that he decided to cup his hands and risk taking a drink even though the water was stagnant and brown. Normally, he reflected, it would be running briskly and clear at this time of year.

How different each season was – not just from season to season, but also from year to year. Spring that year, for example, had been late and then all came in a rush. And each day was unique. Today, with its thunderstorms and rapidly changing light, could only happen at precisely that time of year. It was not tomorrow and it was not yesterday: this particular day had a stamp all of its own and, as he knew from working out in the open, no two days were ever exactly the same. Subtly but surely, the year progressed through its cycle. He stood still and became aware of a silence beyond the chattering birds, sounds of insects and rustlings from the soft breeze.

As he scanned the road, looked under bushes in case the coin had rolled off the road, peered under bridges and logs over streams and gazed up at the magnificent clouds in the sky, Thomas felt a great sense of oneness with everything around him.

The farmhouse came into sight. If there was anywhere he had lost the coin it was likely to be here, in the early stages, but it was nowhere to be found. Somehow, he didn't even particularly mind. He passed the field he had ploughed the day before and saw Castor and Pollux and the cattle and sheep with which he spent so much time. He felt his heart swell: in a strange but real way, he realised the land and the animals were his friends. They were what put him in touch with an inner peace. But there was something else that mattered too.

"What now, Thomas," said his master, "back so early?"

"Aye, indeed," said Thomas. "It was good to be away, but there are more important things than the revelries in town. And – and I would like to be at meeting tomorrow."

# A Troublesome Friend

The Elders had done all they could to discourage Ebenezer Payne from continuing to own slaves. They had spoken gently with him, reasoned with him, even threatened him and, to their own distress and shame, had raised their voices.

"Indeed," confessed William Foster in a low voice to the other Elders of the small Quaker meeting in rural Pennsylvania, "such was the man's stubbornness that only the good Lord prevailed upon my fist to remain by my side and not disfigure his countenance."

"Thou meanest," said Benjamin Walker, who favoured plain speaking, "that it was all thou couldst do, Friend, not to punch him on the nose."

"Such was indeed my sentiment and my favoured course of action and I take no pride in it, but let it be a measure of how mightily provoked I was."

William Foster thought back to the conversation he had had with Ebenezer.

"Thou art a troublesome Friend, Ebenezer," he said severely. "Thou knowst it is no longer considered right for Friends to hold slaves."

"That may be the way the tide of opinion is flowing, William Foster, but tides can also turn. I am not persuaded that what I am doing is wrong, before God or before any man."

"The tide has been flowing for a long time. Nearly a hundred years ago, George Fox said that all were equal before God and we should give slaves their freedom. Thou hast heard what was said at Yearly Meeting in Philadelphia last month."

"What was said at Yearly Meeting is that those who aspire to office in the Society of Friends should not own slaves. I do not aspire to office, Friend."

"Office is not something we aspire to but a duty laid upon us by others in a spirit of discernment. So also must we respect the views of those led by the Spirit, even if we do not agree with them."

"If I give my slaves their freedom I will simply be sending them into far worse bondage. I treat them well. I house them well. I feed them well. Truly do I see that of God in them."

"But true equality means freedom. Freedom is the most precious gift of all."

"I say again: for them freedom is but another name for bondage. They have neither education nor money. Others will take them into slavery or they will find themselves without a roof over their head and with nothing to eat, forced to beg."

"Friend, I say to thee that owning slaves smacks of luxury and makes us appear worldly."

" 'Tis only poor Friends that say so. 'Tis but envy of those of us who are successful."

It was at this point that William Foster had difficulty keeping his fist by his side.

"I fear," said Mary Steer, another of the gathering of Elders, "that reason will get us nowhere. Our Friend William has been provoked to the point of violence and I – I have found myself shouting at him. Oh, how ashamed I was, turning on my heel before Ebenezer could see how I had flushed red."

"There is one other thing we could try," said Elizabeth Clarke, the last of the Elders. "Yearly Meeting agreed to appoint a committee to visit Friends who were still holding slaves. We could write and ask them for Ebenezer to be visited."

Great was the Elders' joy to learn that John Woolman had been appointed to visit Ebenezer. It was the twelfth month of 1758. No other Friend was better known for his opposition to slavery. John Woolman was also deeply respected for his peaceableness and ability to persuade without giving offence.

He was duly received by Ebenezer and Ebenezer's wife Susannah. As it was some distance from Mount Holly where he lived, Woolman arrived late one afternoon to stay the night. Ebenezer was guarded but Susannah, who was a kindly soul, greeted John Woolman warmly.

Refreshments were served. The guest rose to his feet. "And what are the names of these our friends?" he asked, as the servants entered the room.

"Why, this is Abby and this is York," said Suzanne awkwardly.

"My name," said Woolman after a short pause, "is John. John Woolman."

He asked to be taken out to meet another of the slaves, the coachman Jem. They shook hands gravely. John Woolman chatted with him for some time, telling him of his travels and the great city of Philadelphia, and asking about Jem's family and where they had come from. Woolman wished to meet the others, but they were out in the fields. Ebenezer guided him back inside.

"I shall come straight to the point. I know that thou hast come here to persuade me to free my slaves. But look at how the land of Pennsyl-

vania and surrounding states has been opened up! It has all depended on slave labour, and few whites could be found to perform the same work.

"Why," he said, warming to his theme, "the coaches we ride in and the roads we drive on would not be here without them. Our prosperity would not have come about without them. Is it so hard to accept that we are each born into a different station in life?"

Woolman observed that he had come not by coach but on foot. "I have run a tailoring business and my small farm and orchard have prospered without slaves. If as thou sayest we owe our prosperity to these people, then we should set them free and pay them. The labourer is worthy of his hire."

"That is why I treat them well. Indeed they lead far better lives than they would in Africa."

"Friend," replied Woolman, "I rejoice at thy kindness to them. I can not however help feeling uncomfortable when I see the wealth that some people have, such as the silver in this room, when this comes from the unpaid labour of others. We are enjoined towards a tenderness towards all creatures. We are all the sheep of Christ, however different our stations in this world."

"In my experience on this plantation," observed Ebenezer Payne, "the Negro is lazy and slothful. We should not wonder at the differences in wealth."

"Remember, Friend, that the free man finds a satisfaction in cultivating and providing for his family. Those labouring to support others and expecting nothing but slavery during their life lack reason to be industrious. In the love of money it is easy for us to become unmindful of pure wisdom."

Woolman chose his words with care. He spoke of championing the weak, and how Friends had respected and lived in peace with the native Indians in America but had treated the black persons from Africa as inferior. Ebenezer Payne listened closely, and was impressed by the gentle thoughtfulness of his visitor, but could not be persuaded to change his mind.

Upon leaving the next morning, John Woolman handed Ebenezer Payne a small envelope. "I have been well looked after. I should be obliged, Friend Ebenezer, if thou wouldst pass this money to Abby, York, Jem and the others."

Woolman strode off on foot, gravely bidding goodbye to Abby and York at the front door. In his parlour Ebenezer was at a loss.

"This man has no conception of what it means to run a plantation and large house!" he exclaimed to his wife. "What does he imagine I will say to the slaves when I hand over this money? That would look as though I agreed they should be paid – but I cannot keep back the money given by another Friend for so plain a purpose."

The money was handed over, as an expression of thanks, and received with much wonderment. But Ebenezer Payne was a stubborn man and the embarrassment he felt only served to redouble his resolve. Like other wealthy Friends of his acquaintance, he would continue as before.

Once again the Elders met. What now could they do?

"If Ebenezer will not heed one such as our Friend John Woolman, I fear there is nothing more we can do," said Benjamin Walker. "We have set an example, we have reasoned with him, we have cajoled him, we have pleaded with him, we have appealed in a spirit of divine love, we have quoted the Scriptures and the words of George Fox. Alas, Friends, there are some who will not be moved."

"Nay," replied Mary Steer, "but we must try one more time, all of us, in a spirit of charity. We must do so not singly but as one, as the body of Elders."

And so it was that William Foster, Mary Steer, Benjamin Walker and Elizabeth Clarke made their way one evening to the house of Ebenezer and Susannah Payne. A note had been sent beforehand to announce their coming. They pulled on the bell. The front door swung open. They greeted Abby, who led them to the parlour.

They entered the panelled room in such silence that neither Ebenezer nor Susannah felt able to speak. The six Friends sat down. Eyes closed and hands folded, the Elders maintained their silence and a meeting for worship commenced.

The only sound was the slow, steady ticking of the wall-clock. Thirty – or was it forty-five minutes? – passed without a word being said. At length William Foster and Mary Steer shook hands. The visiting Friends rose to their feet and left the parlour in silence. The latch on the front door clicked open and then slipped back into place; the Friends were gone.

Ebenezer and Susannah remained seated in silence in the parlour. It grew dark, but no candle was lit. At last, they each looked up and caught the other's eye.

The slaves were set free.

*   *   *

Here the story might end, but every ending also brings a new beginning. Ebenezer Payne was a stubborn man but, once he changed his mind, he would apply himself to his newly adopted course of action with equal conviction. Each and every one of his slaves was handed a document stating that he or she had been given their freedom, for which payment in full had been made by virtue of the labour they had rendered. Ebenezer spoke at great length with each of them, asking where they would go and what they proposed to do. To those he could offer employment he did so, at fair rates, giving them land on which to build proper housing. He consulted widely with other Friends, persuading some of them to grant his former slaves employment. He and Susannah sold their silver.

Most of all, though, he would remember the time when he first called all his slaves together: the men from the field, the women from the washing tub and the kitchen, the children from their play. They stood in a circle, as the sun was setting. Ebenezer explained, in a few simple words. It had been wrong of him to hold them in bondage. They were all equal, before each other and before God. He was setting them free.

No one moved, and no one spoke.

Once again, it would be difficult to tell how long the silence lasted.

# The Man in White

It rained heavily that summer, the summer of 1763. Walking along the banks of the river Susquehanna in northern Pennsylvania there was a strange party: an Indian man and two Indian women, and two white men. And the older of the two white men really was white! He wore a white beaver skin hat and white, undyed woollen clothes and undressed leather shoes. He was a singular sight and attracted looks wherever he went, from white people, black people and Indian people.

June 1763 was not just unseasonably wet; it was also a time of strife. Officially, the war between England and France had ended some years before, but the fighting against the French in the southern parts of the American colony had inflamed tensions among other white settlers and the native Indian community. The Indians were driven away from the eastern seaboard to more inland areas. The land was less good and it was not so easy to fish. Often, they were forced to live in hilly or rocky parts where the white man could not make a living.

Most of the Indians wanted to get on with their lives as best they could, but in their desperation some of the younger braves began striking out and killing. The white settlers, in turn, began raising forces to deal with them. It was a dangerous time.

It was at this time that the man in white, a tailor and farmer from Mount Holly near Philadelphia, felt the call to travel. His name was John Woolman. There had been Indians in the tiny classroom when he first went to his local school, and he had also come across Indians at meetings with Quakers in Philadelphia. Although he met him only once, one man in particular, an Indian chief called Papunahung, impressed him greatly. Other Friends, too, knew of Papunahung as a man of peace and uncommon wisdom.

It was to Papunahung and the Delaware Indians, almost 200 miles away in north central Pennsylvania, that John Woolman felt called to go. He resisted the call, much as he resisted the initial flutterings to speak in Quaker meetings for worship. But the call would not go away. He discussed it more widely among Friends and received their backing for him to go.

He told his wife Sarah of his plan. It was the custom then for Quakers with a gift for speaking to travel to other communities, on horseback and by foot, but even so she was worried, as it was such an unsafe time to be venturing into Indian territory. But she did not protest, as she was at one with her husband in all things. She knew too that all his life he had been acutely sensitive to inner leadings, and that these were as a great guiding light in his life, and had brought much good, whatever the personal cost. He was one of the few Quakers to take a clear stand against the practice of slavery, which was common even among Quakers at the time. His words and writings commanded widespread respect, and were bringing genuine change. That he should feel a similar understanding and sense of oneness with the native Americans came as no surprise to Sarah. She was a capable woman and she and their thirteen year-old daughter Mary would be able to cope perfectly well for the few weeks that John was away.

One evening shortly before he was due to leave, they had retired for the night when there was an unexpected knocking at the door. Roused from his sleep, John went to the door to be greeted by a messenger, whom he knew. Three Friends, he said, had hurried from Philadelphia specially to see him, and were at the public house in Mount Holly. Hastily he dressed and made his way to the Three Tuns Tavern.

The Friends had come because they knew of his plans and had just learned that Indians to the west had overrun a fort near Pittsburgh, killing and scalping some white settlers. Gravely, he discussed with Sarah the next morning what he had learned. She was greatly concerned. John went into the apple orchard, spending several hours in inward contemplation. When he returned to the house, Sarah knew that his mind was clear. He must go.

\* \* \*

The seed for the journey had been sown two years before when John was visiting some Friends who kept slaves – something that upset him greatly, although he had the rare gift of being able to convey his beliefs gently, without giving offence. He fell in with the company of some trustworthy Indian traders who were about to return to the small Indian settlement of Wyalusing, where Papunahung and his people lived.

Before they got on to more serious subjects, one of the traders, trying to find words that would not appear impolite, remarked that John Woolman was wearing "most unusual clothes".

"It is true. I am afraid that my clothes attract a lot of attention, which I do not seek. To begin with I minded that, but now it no longer concerns me when I am stared at. I just dress as simply as I can, as I know that the dyes used in clothing not only serve to conceal the dirt but often come from the West Indies, where they are produced with the use of slave labour. I reached a point at which I could no longer in good conscience wear clothes that involved the exploitation of other people."

On the subject of exploitation, the traders told Woolman about the practice of selling rum to Indian traders. In a state of intoxication the Indians would often sell precious furs and skins for far below their value, to buy more rum. Woolman listened closely to their account, and then spoke with great feeling and warmth about those who were being harmed, and how also the Indians were often driven off their land without receiving proper payment. None of the Indians listening were left unmoved, including some who spoke no English.

He then hesitantly asked whether it might be possible to travel to Wyalusing and meet Great Chief Papunahung and the Delaware people.

"Why," the traders had asked, "would you want to visit our people?"

"Because, friends, I have long felt love in my heart towards the natives of this land, who now dwell so far back in the wilderness. Their ancestors owned and lived where we now dwell. Yours are a people I admire, and for whose afflictions I grieve. I wish to understand how you live. And I would like to learn from you how you live in the spirit. And perhaps your people might be helped in some degree if I were to follow the leadings of truth among them."

The men marvelled. It was not often that a white settler would consider that the Indians had anything to offer, unless it was something from which he could make a quick financial gain. In turn, John Woolman wanted to know more about Papunahung. He knew a number of things already: that he had once been badly wounded by another

Indian with a tomahawk, but refused to take revenge; that he had prevented a blood feud after an Indian had been murdered by a white man; and that he and the Delawares had refused to join other Indian tribes in a war against the English colonists.

"If I am not mistaken he is a man of great inner peace who has an understanding that goes beyond words," John said. "These are qualities that are not often found, and I am wondering how life brought him to this point."

The men told him that it had not always been so. As a young man, Papunahung was fiery and often difficult. Then his father died, cruelly and unexpectedly. Papunahung took himself off into the forest for several days "in great bitterness of spirit". There, he questioned the Great Spirit who could have allowed this to happen. In his solitude, he entered into the depths of his sadness and anger. He returned a changed man. He gave up violence, practised a calm and meditative way of life and spread a rare sense of love among those with whom he came into contact.

"You are right: he is one of our greatest ever leaders, even though he has won no battles, captured no territory and signed no treaties."

"It is what I saw when he was here," said Woolman, nodding.

* * *

So it was that two years later the small group was making its way along the river Susquehanna. Apart from John Woolman there was another Quaker, Benjamin Parvin who at 36 was John's junior by six years, and three Indian guides. With menacing dark rain clouds gathering, they set up camp earlier than normal. All night it rained steadily. At last, as dawn broke, the rain began to ease. As they all emerged from their tents the three Indians smiled, for they had discovered that the two white men knew more about camping in tents than they did! By piling bracken and bushes beneath the thin blankets on which they slept, John and Benjamin had been able to keep dry when the puddles from the heavy rain seeped beneath the walls of the tent.

They were on an Indian trail. Walking about before breakfast, John Woolman came across some large trees nearby with colourful scenes painted on the trunks where bark had been stripped away. They showed warriors, past conquests and battles, mainly in red and black. It was strange to see these reminders of the former exploits of the peaceable people he was now going to visit. The heroic pictures filled him not with admiration but with sadness.

The small party pressed on and, on a sunny evening, reached the Indian settlement of Wyoming in the back parts of Pennsylvania. People appeared to be hastening out of the settlement and at first they could not find anyone to speak to. At last they found an old man alone in his hut. He told them that two other forts had been attacked to the west. A small group of Indians bearing two English scalps had been seen in a town just ten miles from Wyalusing saying that it was war with the English. So tense was the situation that the sight of the two white men was enough to make the local Indians flee as they entered Wyoming. John Woolman and Benjamin Parvin stood silently in the open doorway of the hut reflecting on what they had been told. The light was beginning to fade.

Beyond the hut they became aware of an Indian moving stealthily in the shadows. Benjamin did not have a good feeling when he spotted him. His first instinct was to grab a weapon or shout for their three Indian guides. But even before he could decide what to do he saw, to his alarm, that John Woolman had walked out of the hut into the clearing. As the Indian's hand went to his coat and pulled out a hatchet, his face contorting into a dreadful grimace, Woolman held out his open hand in greeting and slowly advanced towards the man. He did not smile, knowing that this was not taken as a sincere greeting by the Indians.

So surprising was this gesture that the Indian paused. The sound of John Woolman's soft and gentle words of greeting hung in the early evening air. He explained that he came with a love for the Indian people and that they wanted to learn from them about the Great Spirit. The astonished Indian joined the others in the hut and was soon smoking a pipe and engaged in eager discussion.

The Indians told the two Quakers that carrying on to Wyalusing would be perilous and that they themselves were going to abandon their village for a safer place.

John Woolman could not help but be conscious of the dangers. His health, already not particularly good, had been made worse by the unseasonable wetness and the often mountainous terrain. He wrestled with his soul in the small hours of the night. Benjamin beside him appeared to be asleep but, had Woolman but known it, was secretly awake, aware that the older man was struggling to discern what he should do. Should he go back, and be with Sarah and Mary before the danger spread more widely? Was it fair to expose his loyal companion Benjamin to such risks? True, he had done all he could to dissuade Benjamin from accompanying him, making it plain that he was comfortable undertaking the journey by himself, but Benjamin had a sense of rightness about staying with him that was equal to his own.

At length, going almost as deep within himself as the time when he had come so close to dying two and half years before, he found an inner peace. From the change in his breathing Benjamin knew the decision had been taken, and that they would continue.

In the morning, John Woolman told the twenty or so Indians remaining in Wyoming that they would press on as planned. Soon they encountered more Indians who were fleeing the area. Camping by the river they were caught by a storm of such violence that it beat right through their tent, drenching them and their baggage. Progress was slowed by fallen trees and the slippery, muddy tracks. In the afternoon they came across a party of Indian traders coming downstream from Wyalusing by canoe, who warned them of three Indian warriors on their way to do battle with the English at a nearby settlement, and whom they were almost bound to meet on the trail. Woolman was able to give the traders' leader a letter for posting to his wife, but did not turn back. It was eleven days since they had first set out.

The next day the skies cleared. Aware that they might at any turn meet the three Indian braves, who would be glad to relieve them of their headpieces, they struggled on. John Woolman was feeling unwell but his determination was undiminished, and he retained his inner conviction that they would continue to be watched over. At length they started to come across cultivated fields and houses.

The first person they saw was an Indian woman carrying a baby. She greeted them pleasantly, expressing her gladness at seeing them, and saying that she had heard they were coming. The two Friends sat down on a log in silent thankfulness for having reached Wyalusing. The woman, having first turned away, came back and sat with them. They

stayed together in a deep inward silence while their Indian guide went on to announce their arrival, which was marked by the blowing of a conch-shell.

As the woman said, news of their journey had preceded them. Indeed, it was known for some days that they were coming. A Moravian pastor called David Zeisberger, who was also bound for the community at Wyalusing, had caught up with Woolman and his companions in the course of their journey. They had already passed through the Moravian town of Bethlehem, and word got out that a Quaker party was bound for Wyalusing, where the Moravians had previously had some contact. While he did not say so, it appeared that the Pastor was intent on reaching the Indians before the Quakers. Woolman was not interested in making converts and decided to take a day of rest and allow the Pastor to press on by himself.

Chief Papunahung was aware of the two differing traditions in his midst and wished to avoid any discord. He knew the Quakers and was familiar with their way of worship, but did not wish to offend his Moravian visitor, who was a kind and good man with a genuine love for the Indian people. It was agreed that religious gatherings would be held in the Moravian tradition, but that Woolman might speak if he felt so moved.

Six such gatherings, attended each time by about sixty people, were held. At the first Woolman spoke, with power and authority. His task was, however, made difficult by the fact that the Pastor's English was limited and that interpretation was required into both German and the Delaware tongue. In the end he told the interpreters that he would say a few words to God in prayer, without need for them to translate, and the spirit of harmony hung over the meeting. When the service was over, he noticed that one of the interpreters was attempting to provide Papunahung with a summary. But Papunahung smiled and held up his hands to stop the man talking: "I love to feel where words come from."

John Woolman ministered again in the second gathering on the second day, which was a Sunday. He spoke of the pure light which enlightened every person coming into the world. It was to the guidance of that light that they should all attend. He spoke of the equality of all people, and took the opportunity to explain why his clothes – now washed – were of such an unusual nature. He spoke of the change that could occur in people's lives, and of real beauty and true harmony. They were known rightly only to those who had borne the Cross of their own lives, facing the weaknesses and light within.

Woolman and Papunahung were able to spend some time together in the place where words come from and where there are no words. Afterwards, Papunahung would say that never had he felt such a sense of shared communion with the divine. And this with a man who was to say that he felt less worthy than many of the people in Papunahung's community. "Mark this man," he told his people, "we have a great spirit in our midst. He sees the equalness of all people, is open to the suffering of those he does not know, and lives his life in the fullness of his beliefs, whatever the cost. The light that streams out of him comes from that one great source of light. He is not protected against the divine like most of us. It is as though there is nothing between him and the Sun. He is as a tree without its bark, a deer without its hide."

Woolman and Parvin were anxious about retracing their steps through the ever more dangerous Indian territory, but when they left on the fourth day they found they were not alone. They were joined by a group of twenty or so Indian traders, laden with hides and furs. They came not just to afford the two white men protection, but also because they knew that Woolman and Benjamin could ensure their protection in Bethlehem.

The party travelled by canoe, the horses being led separately along paths by the river. They passed through Wyoming again, forded the Delaware River on three occasions to avoid crossing the Blue Mountains as they had done on the outward journey, and killed four rattlesnakes. Each evening, there would be a time of shared silence after the meal. On reaching Bethlehem they calmed the fears of the local people concerning the Indian traders, about whom they were at first much alarmed. There the group parted with dignity and affection.

John and Benjamin continued on their journey, one day later going their separate ways. Another day and John Woolman was home. Sarah and Mary were well. He had been taught patience, he had become even more aware the sufferings of others, and he knew that if he had come home safely, it was not of his doing but came from that place beyond words.

# The Lone Preacher

The logging camp was empty. The tall, distinguished-looking traveller was puzzled. He wandered around the log cabin in the middle of the clearing. "Anybody 'ome?" he called out.

The words rang out among the trees, carrying just the hint of a foreign accent. The stranger went round the other side of the building and called out again. Once again there was silence except for the murmurings of the breeze in the lofty trees. He peered into the lean-to shed at the end of the log cabin, but apart from some sawn timber and a few tools it was empty.

The man tied up his tired and dusty horse to a tree beside the stream in the valley. He pushed open the door to the log cabin and found himself in a gloomy space with a rough table, one or two barrels and a few crudely made wooden chairs.

He sat down on one of the barrels, his back perfectly straight. He closed his eyes. For perhaps half an hour or even an hour – who could tell? – he remained silent and motionless. At last he got to his feet.

"Friends," he said in a loud, clear voice, "thank you for allowing me to join you in meeting for worship. I have travelled by myself on horseback for three days to be with you. You may not be here, but I feel your spirits with me. And there is Another Presence with us as well.

"My name is Stephen Grellet. That is a French name, and you may wonder how, as a Frenchman, I have appeared in your midst as a Quaker. You will know of Quakers since this state of Pennsylvania was founded by that great Quaker William Penn. But how does a Frenchman come to be travelling in the ministry, to share with you in this forest the truth of the Inward Light that is in us all? And I am a Frenchman whose childhood was the very opposite of the Quaker values of equality and simplicity.

"Who I am is unimportant, except for how my life has turned out so very differently from what I expected. I was born into a wealthy,

aristocratic French family. We lived in a small castle or chateau with a magnificent garden, I was always dressed in the finest of fashions, we had a huge team of servants and there were splendid balls at which whole orchestras would play.

"When I was sixteen the French Revolution broke out. I went to fight for the King but when it was clear that the cause was lost my two brothers and I had to flee for our lives. Our parents were imprisoned and, I later learned, very nearly died. In great danger we managed to make our way to Amsterdam in Holland. From there I went to Demerara in Dutch Guiana with my brother Joseph. We lived there for two years, running a business, but I was shocked by many things there, especially the terrible slavery.

"And so, just over fifteen years ago in 1795, I came to New York, settling in Long Island. We were lonely and dejected. We spoke very little English. I had lost all belief in God.

"A kind family who spoke French had taken us in. One evening I was walking in the fields. I had no religious thoughts: on the contrary, life seemed to have lost all meaning. And then, out of nowhere, there came a voice. I could hear it, but not with my ears; it came from outside me, and yet was also within. *'Eternité! Eternité! Eternité!'* the voice said. The words shook my very soul, and I fell to the ground.

"That moment was to change my life. It came to me unasked and it was as though something vast was cracked open before me. Before, I had been shutting myself away; now, I knew there were great worlds beyond me that I could never understand but which meant everything. I knew there was a light within each of us, and that if we could but follow it we would know what was right for us in our lives. That one word – eternity! – said everything.

"I wanted to read. I *needed* to read. Now, I realise that we must just accept and be aware but then I wanted to make sense of what had happened to me. In the library of the house where I was staying I found a copy of *No Cross No Crown* by William Penn. Even though my English was so poor the truth of his words pierced me to the core. Soon afterwards, my brother and I were invited to attend a Quaker meeting. My brother Joseph found it very boring but I found in me what I had so long, and with so many tears, sought outside of me. That, my Friends, is how I came to Quakerism – from a life of luxury, violence and godlessness.

"Since then I have travelled a great deal, trying to share some of what has been opened up to me. I have tried to share what I know of the light that guides us all. I have drawn on those times of luxury and the terrible way that the poor in France were treated, as well as my experience of having seen the wickedness of slavery at first hand. I have been shocked to find that even Quakers in this country have slaves and I have brought the message to western Virginia and elsewhere that we must see God in these people too and do what we can to grant them a full life. I knew too that I should visit the sick in Philadelphia suffering from yellow fever. I myself fell ill. When people had given up hope of my recovery, once again I heard the inner voice telling me that I was not to die and that my work was not yet done.

"And why am I here? I am here because I am obeying the same promptings that have so changed my life. I heard of your camp, and that some of you had been in trouble with the law. The idea would not leave me that I should visit you. It has taken me much time and effort to find you, and I am wondering why I should have been brought to this place only to find that you are gone. But perhaps the meaning will be revealed to me at some point. What is important is for us to remain faithful and true to what we know deep within."

The preacher warmed to his theme and continued talking about the equality of all people and about ordering our lives in tune with the inward sense of the divine. Even though nobody was there, Stephen Grellet felt that he had never spoken better. In later years he was often to draw on the words that came to him that day, but never again, he felt, did he speak with such power and conviction.

"A Quaker meeting is like an orchestra, such as I used to hear make music in my father's chateau. Our music, though, is that of silence. Each one of us contributes to the silence, like instruments together produce the sound made by an orchestra. Sometimes, one of us will feel moved to stand and speak, much as a single instrument in the orchestra – a violin, or trumpet – will play a solo. We do not, however, have a conductor, and there is no score; we make up the music, deeper than silence, as we go along."

It troubled him, though, that he had come all that way only to find the camp empty. Where was the orchestra, why was he a one-man band? The inward voice had never let him down; why should he have been brought to this place for no purpose? Out loud he heard himself saying that it was not for us to question what we were doing but to be true to our leadings. He was, he admitted, struggling with this strange event, but reminded his unseen audience that it was human of us to doubt, to question and to be challenged. "Look not for certainty, Friends. Ask not where the path is taking you. It is enough to know that you are on that path."

He sat down. There followed another long period of silence. At last, Stephen Grellet rose to his feet and looked out through the slits cut into the sides of the log cabin. He was still alone: more alone than he had perhaps ever been and yet, strangely, as close to all around him as he had ever felt.

He stayed the night at the camp and then, when no one had appeared by mid-morning, he reluctantly saddled up his horse again and rode back down the track, crossing streams and guiding his horse carefully down steep rocky parts, until at last he reached the little settlement where four days before he had hired the horse.

\* \* \*

Six years later Stephen Grellet visited London. His calling was to tend to French soldiers captured in the war against Napoleon and held in prison in London. In the course of his ministry he visited Newgate Prison, where he was shocked by the conditions in which he saw the women prisoners were being held. They were like caged animals, half naked and shrieking.

During his time in London he was introduced to a Quaker woman, Elizabeth Fry, and it was to her that he turned with his account of the conditions in the prison. Deeply moved, she managed to persuade the governors of the prison to let her in and speak with the women. Her ministry in the prison was to last for many years and have a great effect on prison conditions throughout the country.

All that, however, lay far into the future. Late in the afternoon after he had visited Newgate Prison, Stephen Grellet found himself standing on London Bridge. He was lost in contemplation, staring out over the River Thames without really taking in all the sights on the water. All at once he became aware of a short, stocky man by his side looking at him keenly.

"Forgive me," he said, in an American accent, "but aren't you the man who preached a sermon all by himself in that log cabin in Pennsylvania six years ago?"

Steven looked at him in surprise. "I am! But, as you say, I was all by myself – so how do you know I was there?"

"I was one of the log cutters. We had decided to work in a different part of the forest for a few days. I came back to collect some tools we had forgotten. As I approached the log cabin I heard a voice ringing out. I was astonished. Peering through a crack between the timbers I saw a lone figure standing in the room, preaching a sermon in the empty space. The words you spoke changed my life. Later, I went back to the others and told them what you had said. Since then, I have been sharing what I learned that day with anyone who will listen."

# The Woman in Grey

"Granny, tell us about the quilt and Elizabeth Fry!"

"Oh, Milly, it was such a long time ago."

"*Please,* Granny," the three girls chorused. Milly, Amy and Harriet had Grandma all to themselves for the whole afternoon. They always loved the story about Elizabeth Fry. Lying on a rug on the grass one autumn day in Parramatta just outside Sydney, they were determined to extract every last detail from their grandmother. She was sitting in a rocking chair out in the garden, with a quilt over her knee, even though it was not particularly cold. The year was 1860.

"Well," said Grandma briskly, "we shall need some lemonade – you run to the kitchen Amy, and get four glasses – and we shall need some more cushions, which is a job for you Harriet. And you, Milly, can help me move the rug into the shade."

When they were all settled, Grandma began. "You see, Milly, it all began when I was just your age – thirteen. We didn't come from London but moved there, like so many people, from the country. We thought we would have a better life there. I was about eleven or twelve then. There was your great-grandfather Eric and your great-grandmother Amelia – after whom you are named, Amy – and then five of us children. I was the eldest, and then there were Peter, Frank, Betsy and Mary.

"But things did not go well when we moved to London. We lived in a single, damp and dingy room in a poor part of London. We missed the village life. The first winter was terrible. We all huddled together in the one bed and yet we still couldn't keep warm. Eric – my father – developed a cough. He worked in the docks, loading and unloading ships. Often there wasn't enough work and it was all we could do to make ends meet. But his cough got worse and a little over a year after moving to London he died.

"My mother was desperate. Betsy was always a sickly child and my mother thought seriously about going back to the country, except that it would have been even more difficult for her to find work there. She managed to take in some laundry and also worked as a seamstress, making and mending clothes. Peter, Frank and I did what we could to help her, but Betsy and Mary were still too little.

"As the eldestI needed to find work and I got a position as a scullery maid in a big house. But the master of the house died in 1815 at the Battle of Waterloo and sometime later the house was sold and I had no job.

"Winter was coming on, and Betsy was coughing like our father used to. Mother was exhausted, and Frank was such a high-spirited and troublesome child. Sometimes when the others were asleep my mother would speak to me in a low voice, confiding her fears and worries.

"One day there was ice on the streets. I didn't even have any shoes but went out to taverns and other places I knew, where people would sometimes be looking for servants. I was hungry, tired and cold. The shops had closed because it was dark. I was walking through those new streets in Bloomsbury when a horse and carriage came round the corner too quickly and clipped the bow-windowed front of one of the shops.

"One window was smashed. The carriage didn't stop and nobody seemed to have noticed what had happened. I peered in through the hole in the window. It was a shop that sold silver. With a stick I was able to pull a candlestick towards me across the table and reach in. I knew it was wrong, but also knew somewhere I could sell it and I knew how much the money would mean to us all.

"Just as I was trying to hide the candlestick under my clothes a man came round the corner. It was the shop owner. He growled at me and I ran off in fright but a coachman at the end of Woburn Place saw what was happening and grabbed me, handing me over to the shop owner."

Grandma paused. The girls all stayed silent. They had never heard Grandma tell her story in such detail before.

"The law is a strange thing. If, like me, you were caught stealing something from a shop but had not been seen in the act you could be sentenced to hang, whereas if you had been seen you could only be sent to prison – which meant being transported off to Australia by ship.

"Soon after I went on trial in the Old Bailey. It was a terrifying place. I was held in a room with seven or eight other people all awaiting trial. Some of the trials lasted no more than ten minutes. We were told that the judge had already sentenced four people to death that day when my turn came in the afternoon, just after the judge had returned from a long lunch.

"My trial did not take long either. The facts were presented very quickly and I was totally tongue-tied. I was found guilty, as I knew I would be. Then came the sentence. I looked up in terror at the judge. Out of the corner of my eye I could see my mother, her face white as snow.

" 'Maude Wilkins,' the judge said in a voice like ice, 'You knew what you were doing, and there is no excuse. You have acted with an art and contrivance beyond your years. I am minded to make you my fifth example for the day, for anything less than hanging would be to reward your wrong-doing and encourage others that they could commit such a crime with impunity. Alas, you are of too tender years.'

"I saw the judge's hand pushing away the black cap that they put on when sentencing people to death. My legs gave way and I fainted. When I came to I found myself being dragged into Newgate Prison. I later learned that I had been sentenced to imprisonment in Australia for fourteen years."

"Fourteen years," exclaimed Milly. "You never told us that before, Granny."

"No," said Grandma quietly, "but you are all old enough now to know more of what happened.

"I cannot describe what it was like in Newgate. The women's part of the prison consisted of five rooms and an infirmary for the sick – not long before there had been just two, so this was an improvement – and a courtyard. I was flung by the turnkeys into the courtyard. Even though it was cold it was full of half-naked, screaming and shouting women. Some of them were fighting. One or two were gambling over cards. One enormous, red-faced woman was dragging another around by the hair. There was a strong smell of gin and some of the women were slumped in a heap on the cold ground. The stench, even outside, was so dreadful you could hardly breathe.

"The huge red-faced woman let go of her victim and started to come towards me, leering alarmingly. I pretended I hadn't seen her and scampered off into one of the rooms. There was hardly any room anywhere and a hideous looking woman screamed 'Be uff with ye!', but another girl my age pointed to a spot on the floor where I was able to curl up under the pitiful pile of rags that was to pass as my bed. Her name was Jenny; she and I were to become inseparable, until people thought we were twins. Jenny, like me, had been sentenced to transportation."

"What had she done?" asked Milly.

"She had stolen a cambric handkerchief."

"Just one handkerchief, Grandma?" said Harriet.

"Yes, dear, just one small handkerchief. That was all it took. And although it was wrong I am glad she *did* take it, or I should have been utterly alone. Life in that place was all but unbearable.

"We had to fight for food and for water. It was impossible to wash. Our hair and clothes grew stiff with dirt. Many people fell ill. Some even died. Every week or so the bell of St Stephens would toll as a group of prisoners would be taken off to be hanged. Far from being shocked many of the women would cheer or jeer at the sight.

"There were lots of children in the prison. Some were very little, there with their mothers, while others like me – and there were lots younger – were there as prisoners. We were a wild, neglected lot.

"Some of the women had money or would find other ways of getting favours from the guards. Some gave birth to babies in the prison. And the noise! There was a constant wailing, screaming and shouting that lasted right through the night. I felt that this could not be true and that I was going mad; some people did go mad.

"One of the most terrifying things was the red-faced giant. She was called Sarah Harps and everyone was frightened of her because she was so violent. There were others who were almost as bad. They forced us to do things for them.

"Worst of all, I learned that I might be there for many months before being transported to Australia – and, from what we knew, the journey by ship and life in Australia were almost as bad as Newgate. Ours was a god-forsaken place of fear, despair, dreadful sadness and lack of all hope. Oh my children, how I hope that you never have to face anything like that."

Grandma took a long sip of lemonade. Everyone was very quiet. Harriet was in tears. Grandma gathered her up on her knee.

"But then something happened," she said, her voice taking on an altogether different, softer sound. "One day someone in the courtyard shouted 'Visitor!'

"We did get visits from time to time, from important-looking men who would look around gravely. This time it was a Frenchman, called I think Stephen Grellet. He had come over from America, where he now lived, to help French soldiers in our prisons. He spent a long time in both halves of the prison, and was one of the very few people who ever spoke to us women. Or tried to speak to us, for some of the women set up a dreadful caterwauling and began throwing mud and rags at him. He took no notice and seemed determined to hear what we had to say, in a way that impressed us. He was clearly shocked at what he saw."

"Did you speak to him, Grandma?" asked Harriet.

"I did," she replied. "He asked me how old I was and why I was in prison. I said I was thirteen and that I had stolen a candlestick because we had no money. He did not condemn me but gave me a look of such pity and kindness, saying 'Poor child, only thirteen.'

"'Please, please do something to help us,' I implored him. 'This is the worst, most dreadful place anyone could ever be in.'

"It was just a day or two later that we received another visitor. Once again the cry went up in the courtyard. This time, though, it was a woman. We had never had a lady visitor before. I was in the courtyard with Jenny when the lady was brought in by the turnkeys. I heard one of them saying to her in a low voice, 'Ma'am, I implore you, this is not a good idea. They're just animals, they are. Give 'em half a chance and they'll tear the very clothes off your back, they will. It's not safe for you to go in.'

"But she would have none of it. 'Just let me pass, I shall be perfectly all right, thank you,' she said briskly. We all quickly gathered round. Sarah Harps pushed her way over to her menacingly. Some of the women began jeering and jostling; others began picking up clods of mud.

"But there was something about the woman that made people hold back. She was tall and dressed not in the usual finery of the day but in a simple grey silk dress with a white cap. There was an assurance about her that commanded respect, a kind of inner resolve. There were Sarah and the others bent on causing mischief, and yet she looked at them so calmly and kindly that they just stood there and let her pass. Somehow, I knew that she, like the Frenchman, was on our side.

"The woman asked if she might speak to us all. Jenny produced a chair, but she said, 'Thank you, my dear young lady, but either we all sit down, which we can't in this mud, or we all stand up.

" 'Friends, my name is Elizabeth Fry,' she went on. 'I am here because of what I have been told. I see that many of us are mothers. I too am a mother.' Suddenly, everyone was listening intently. She went on to say how heartbreaking it was to see children brought up in conditions like that and how they deserved better and how there was so much that we could all do. She never said 'you' but always 'we'. She insisted on being shown where we slept and what we had to eat. I saw anger spread over her face when she was told that all we got was a scrap of bread once a day unless we had money to buy something more.

" 'We need straw for bedding, and soup. I shall arrange for them to be delivered, my friends. And we need a school for the children, where they can learn to read and write.'

"In fact, not just the children but nearly all the adults were unable to read and write. When she left us we felt, for the very first time, a sense of hope. Some of the older and wiser ones called a meeting. Everyone came. Somehow we all crowded into the largest room, which was the laundry we never used. Was there anyone who could read and write properly and who could teach the others?

"A young woman called Mary Connor shyly stepped forward. We all knew her as a quiet person who kept out of trouble. She was one of the very few people Jenny and I ever dared speak to. Now and then she would even share with us some of the cheese and sausage she managed to buy. She would have to do so very secretly, or the food would have been snatched out of her hands by the likes of Heartless Harps, as we called her behind her back. Any sign of pity or helpfulness was normally pounced on.

"But Elizabeth Fry had somehow changed the atmosphere, just by her one visit. True to her word she had straw delivered for bedding and a huge tureen of soup appeared, with proper bowls for it to be served out in. When she herself came on her next visit you should have seen how proud we were to tell her that we had chosen someone to be the schoolteacher.

"There were Bible readings. Oh, my children, if I could just convey to you her voice when she read those passages to us. It was like the clearest of bells. Many of us had never heard anything from the Bible before. Now I know it well, and can see the care with which she chose readings that were so right for us. Often, the most hardened women would be reduced to tears.

"Everyone came to the readings, and it was also soon clear that the adults, just as much as the children, wanted education. We set about with great busyness turning one of the rooms into a school, but it soon turned out to be too small. So the laundry was turned into a school room. We had a meeting at which we all agreed to certain rules. We were to dress properly and there was to be no violence or bad language. Materials would be provided for us to work with. All this, however, was not forced on us, and we were asked every step of the way whether we agreed. We were told that women would be coming in but that they would not be in authority over us and giving us commands; instead, we would all be acting together and by agreement. Above all, she made us feel that we – the dregs of society – were decent and worthwhile people. She also taught us the Quaker belief of seeing that of God in everyone. Those words were like rain falling on parched soil."

"Did you ever speak to Mrs Fry?" asked Milly. She knew the answer, but wanted to make sure that her younger sisters heard too.

"I did," said Grandma. "It was very early on – the second or third visit, I think. She came over to Jenny and me and asked whether it was one of us who had spoken to Stephen Grellet. I confess that such was the kindness and concern I felt from her presence that I burst into tears. I found myself pouring out my heart to her. It was like a dam that had burst. Apart from dear Jenny there had been no no-one I could talk to. But there was something so trusting about her, a kind of inner stillness as well as great strength. The words came tumbling out, about the fear and the food and the cold and the smell, about the harshness and savagery and drunkenness and shame. I told her about my mother and my brothers and sisters and how I missed them terribly and how deeply ashamed I was about what had happened.

"She told me I had nothing to be ashamed about. She said that I was a fine and good young woman. She spoke so warmly to Jenny as well. When she realised how distressed I was about my family she asked me for my mother's address. That very day she called on my mother to tell her that I was all right. She came back the next day with a message from my mother saying how proud she was of me and how much they all missed and loved me. I shall never forget Mrs Fry's kindness.

"Everyone in that dreadful place was transformed. It was a miracle. The solemn-looking men who came to visit us from time to time were visibly astonished at the change. They made notes in their little books. They even spoke to some of us, as we were no longer like wild animals. Everyone was neatly dressed and the place was orderly. No one drank or gambled any more. We all helped one another and took a pride in our work and our progress at school. Mary Connor was a won-derful teacher."

"And what about the quilt, what about the patchwork quilt!" said Amy impatiently. "Tell us about the quilt."

"One the most important things was that we were given work. This gave us something to do and a sense of purpose. All sorts of scraps of material were brought in by the Quaker women and we worked these up into patchwork quilts. These were much in demand in New South Wales, where we were being sent, and so we would have at least a little bit of money when we got there. We also made knitted goods and stockings.

"I was good at needlework as I had learned it from my mother. I helped Jenny with her quilt. I sold mine when we arrived in New South Wales but, years later, found it for sale in a shop. So it came back to me, and here it is now, on my knee."

"What happened to Jenny?" asked Amy.

"Jenny was released after serving her sentence and married a man with whom she returned to England. But I, as you know, met and married your dear grandfather and stayed on here in New South Wales."

"When did you leave the prison for New South Wales, Gran?" asked Harriet.

"That was not until the summer of the following year, but at last word came that we were to be taken to the ship that was to carry us to Australia. My heart was almost breaking at the thought that we should no longer see Mrs Fry and all the women who came into the prison so regularly. Mrs Fry insisted to the authorities that we not be carted in irons to the docks like dangerous beasts. Instead, we were to go in closed hackney coaches. She came to visit us at Newgate the night before we left and read to us at great length from the Bible. Instead of the usual riots and commotion at such a time we were all greatly comforted and, somehow, strangely confident that all would be well.

"Our ship was called the *Maria*. It remained moored in the river for six weeks before sailing. As with the prison we smartened it up as best we could and continued to run the school and to work at our quilts and the other handiwork. Mrs Fry often came to see us that summer while we were waiting to sail. She would read to us on the open deck, and the sailors would stop and listen.

"Then, at last, we got news that we would be sailing. Elizabeth Fry came one last time. I remember she read the 23rd Psalm, the Lord is my shepherd. After the words 'He leadeth me beside the still waters', she stopped for a moment. I think we all prayed then that the waters of the journey and in the rest of our lives would be still. Then she took her leave of us, one by one. I was so overcome that I cannot remember her last words to me, but it did not matter; I knew that she saw me for myself. I could stand up straight as Maude Wilkins and be proud of myself. And, like Mrs Fry had shown us, I now could see the good in all the other women rejected by society as worthless. How they had all changed, and how much they all meant to me!

"Mrs Fry climbed over the side and took her place in the little skiff that was to carry her back to shore, and we all leant over the side to wave her off. As the rowing boat pulled away one voice, full of emotion but clear, uttered words that I have never forgotten:

"'Our prayers will follow you – and a convict's prayers will be heard.'

There was a pause. Then Milly asked, "Do you remember who it was who spoke those words, Grandma?"

"Yes, dearest. It was Sarah Harps."

# A Friend to Slaves

The heavy doors swung open. The brocade curtains were pulled aside. Even though he set no store by finery or rank, Thomas Clarkson's heart beat faster. Here, on this late summer's evening in Paris, he was in the presence of one of the most powerful men in Europe, Tsar Alexander I of Russia.

The Tsar put him at his ease. He asked about the slave trade, and all that Clarkson had done to bring about its end in Britain eight years before, in 1807. In his uncomplicated, direct way, he told the Tsar of his anguish about the treatment of the African people taken in slavery, and how the fight against the slave trade had taken over his life. Much still remained to be done in other countries.

The Tsar was well-informed and asked intelligent questions, and clearly needed no convincing of the injustice of slavery. On the table beside him was a complete set of Clarkson's works on the slave trade.

They spoke for an hour. Suddenly, the Tsar leant forward. "Are you a Quaker?" he enquired.

"I am not a Quaker in name, Sire, but I would hope in spirit, for I am nine parts in ten of their way of thinking. They have laboured with me in this great cause, and the more I have known them, the more I have loved them."

Putting his hand to his heart, the Russian Emperor declared: "I embrace them more than any other people; I consider myself as one of them."

Thomas could not conceal his surprise and asked the Tsar whether he had met many Quakers.

"Last year, when I was in London, I attended a Quaker meeting. Afterwards, three Friends came to see me: William Allen, John Wilkinson and Stephen Grellet. I have the most agreeable memories of the occasion. They kept their hats firmly on their heads all the time," the Tsar chuckled.

Thomas could not help laughing. "It was fortunate for them it was not some other monarch, or their heads might have been cut off, hat and all!"

The Tsar too laughed but then, with a faraway look in his eye, observed, "From reading your works, Thomas Clarkson, I am only too aware that many a slave lost his head for far less of an offence. By keeping on their hats, our Friends in London were saying that we are all equal before our Maker. It is because we do not regard the slaves as equal that this great evil exists."

\* \* \*

Hearing this story from my Uncle Harry, who had heard it himself from Thomas Clarkson, took me back to the time in my boyhood when he had first told me about Thomas Clarkson.

Uncle Harry was the most interesting person in our family. He had been to sea. He had been involved in the slave trade. He had visited exotic places such as the Gold Coast and the Caribbean. And now he was a clerk of buildings at one of the colleges in Cambridge, where he was a byword for always wearing his black Quaker hat. Uncle Harry, my father's older brother, was at that time the only Quaker in the family.

Uncle Harry was also the most mysterious member of our family. I knew, for example, not to ask him anything about slaves. Once, when I had done so as a small boy, a strange look passed over his face and our conversation came to an abrupt end.

Then, some years later when I was nearly thirteen, I found Uncle Harry in a state of great excitement. "Parliament has abolished the slave trade!" he exclaimed. It was the year 1807.

"There are things that have been too dreadful for me to share with you, Tom, but you are old enough now, and besides, it is right for you to understand what Parliament has done. The world will not be the same again."

Uncle Harry had gone to sea at the age of 18. We lived in Bristol then, where my grandfather was a cabinet-maker. My father followed in his footsteps but Uncle Harry could not resist the lure of the tall ships.

"I would be gone for many months at a time. We plied what was known as the triangle trade: down to the west coast of Africa to pick up slaves, across the Atlantic to Jamaica and then back to Bristol with a cargo of sugar or cotton.

"You must understand that slavery was perfectly normal then, just a quarter of a century ago. I didn't give it a second thought. It was not that we had to become hardened; we were already hardened. But by about the third trip you could say that I started to become 'softened up'.

"For weeks and sometimes months on end we would go up and down the coast of West Africa, picking up a single slave here and two or three there, until we had a full load. We transported them as though they were cattle, packing them below decks so that they could barely move. In the intense tropical heat, the stench was overpowering: the vomit and all the rest, and the sweat and blood of those wretched human beings seeped into the very woodwork. You could smell a slave vessel a mile downwind.

"Sometimes we had to go down below to shackle or unshackle someone or to haul out a dead body. It was all but impossible to stay below decks among the slaves for more than a few minutes.

"But since I could read and write, I rose to become second mate. The pay was not good but I was also able to do some trading on my own account, taking out trinkets from England and then trading them for African goods such as ivory, beeswax and beautiful cotton textiles, which I would sell in Jamaica. So I did well financially, and largely kept my misgivings to myself.

"The turning point came when I signed up on a ship by the strange name of *Zong*. We took a long time picking up a full load of slaves in Africa, and then made very slow progress in light airs and headwinds. It was normal for anything up to a fifth of the slaves to die on the crossing, but this was worse than anything I had seen before. Nearly all of the slaves were severely weakened well before we reached Jamaica. It was clear that the slaves would be virtually worthless when we arrived. The voyage would be a financial disaster.

"It was then that Captain Collingwood came up with a devilish plan. He decided to throw a lot of the slaves overboard, on the grounds that water was beginning to run short, although this was not true. He could then claim insurance on the slaves, in the same way that you could claim insurance on cargo you had to throw overboard in order to save the ship.

"That was the point at which something inside me snapped. I shall never forget the looks on the slaves' faces. One or two of them broke free, but where could they go? There was nowhere for them to hide, and they were soon whipped or pushed with wooden poles into the sea. I felt ashamed to be a human being. In all we cast 132 of the poor unfortunates overboard.

"After this, I fell ill just as we reached Jamaica. Many of the crew suffered from sickness. Conditions on board were so bad that many of the sailors too died in the slave trade. It was quite impossible to stop the terrible sickness among the slaves from spreading to the rest of us. But in my case I knew that I was suffering from a much deeper sickness, a sickness of the soul.

"I was so weak from vomiting and fever and had lost so much weight that I was unable to join the *Zong* for the return journey but stayed behind in Jamaica. I was carried off the ship on a stretcher. As we reached the gangplank Captain Collingwood, whom I had never liked, came across. He muttered something gruffly about how difficult it would be to find another mate for the journey and grudgingly wished me a speedy recovery.

"Summoning what little strength I had I sat half upright and, looking him in the eye as best I could, said, 'Captain Collingwood, what you have done to these people is very wrong. My only comfort is that one day you will have to answer for your actions before God.'"

"What did the captain say?" I asked my uncle.

"I do believe that if I had not been so weak and feeble he would have had me whipped. He swore and cursed and all but kicked me down the gangplank, stretcher and all.

"My health had been so severely undermined that at the advice of a local doctor I spent some time in Jamaica before returning home. I spent nearly a year in Jamaica. Once again my reading and writing and proficiency with numbers came to my aid, and I obtained a job as a clerk in a warehouse. The climate, though hot, suited me, I had pleasant lodgings and there were many people from England, Scotland and Ireland who provided good company.

"As I recovered my strength I made it my business to see as much of this beautiful island as I could. My work took me to many plantations. Here, I would see a side of slave life that those making official visits would never see. People from England inspecting conditions in the plantations would only be shown the lodgings of slaves in superior positions – the carpenters, blacksmiths and tally clerks. What they did not see was the terrible poverty of the cane cutters – most of them women. They would not see the way in which the sugar mills kept working through the night and how slaves were often injured or even killed in the furnaces. They would not see the terrible food they were given. They would not see how sometimes late at night the slaves would simply sink to the earth and fall asleep, too tired even to make their way to the hovels in which they lived.

"What affected me most of all was to see the savage punishments they received for even the slightest mistake, like letting a pot boil over."

Uncle Harry paused. I knew that there was a lot more he could have said. He went over to his desk and extracted some objects from the drawer. There was a thumbscrew, leg shackles and a hideous iron mask: implements which, to this day, haunt me.

"I saw just how cruel and unfeeling human beings can be towards one another. Sometimes slaves who were married would be sold separately and the husband and wife – and children, if there were any – might never see one another again. The hard-heartedness and selfishness reminded me of the *Zong* and caused me much anguish. I became reluctant to mix with other white people outside of my work, even though they were often agreeable company.

"Then, one day, I visited a trading establishment run by a Quaker, Robert King. Most unusually, his chief clerk was a slave. He spoke excellent English and we fell into conversation. He had been snatched away from his village in Senegal as a boy and had had a number of masters, some of whom had been extremely cruel. I shall never forget his words:

"'Whatever they may have done, the dealers in slaves are born no worse than other men,' he said. 'No! It is this mistaken greed, this lust for profit, that corrupts them. Had their life taken a different course, they might have been as generous, as tender-hearted, and as just as they are unfeeling and cruel. This traffic in slaves spreads like a plague and taints what it touches!'

"His words made me look at the white community through different eyes, and made me realise too how people can still forgive even when they have been terribly mistreated."

"Was it because the slaves were so badly treated that you came back to England, Uncle Harry?" I asked.

"It was. Once I had fully regained my strength I quickly found a position on a ship returning to England, making it clear that I would not be staying with the ship after we got back. We made a slow but safe crossing. As soon as we had berthed in Bristol I signed off and returned to see the family. I resolved never to go to sea again.

"Our reunion was a joyous one, but it was short-lived. Several days after I had returned I was seized at night by the crimps and taken on board a ship."

"What are crimps?"

"Ships often have difficulty finding enough sailors. It is dangerous, hard and poorly paid work. If a ship is about to sail and does not have enough crew they will employ gangs to go out and find people. Often they drag them out of taverns when they have had too much to drink. I had gone to an inn with some old friends to celebrate my safe return. The crimps dragged me out of the door, flung me on board and when I sobered up the next morning I found myself on a ship that had already put to sea. I think that Captain Collingwood may have been behind my capture.

"The ship was called the *Fly*. It was a slave ship and sailed the triangle run. I was closely watched at every port in Africa and the West Indies to make sure I did not jump ship, but once we reached Bristol four months later they knew they could not hold me against my will any longer.

"Just as I was disembarking an unusually tall young man in clerical dress asked if he might come aboard. He introduced himself as the Reverend Mr Clarkson. You share the same Christian name with him, Thomas, and you may be proud of that, for it has been Thomas Clarkson, more than anyone else, who has been responsible for changing the way we all think about slavery and making this day possible.

"He sought details on the slave trade. I did not want to linger a moment further, but he had such an air of determination and such a look in his eye as to make me hesitate. When he told me that he had never managed to set foot on a slave vessel, I agreed to show him quickly over the ship, and there was no-one to stop me as the captain had already gone ashore.

"I shall never forget how he fell silent when he saw the cramped, air-less quarters in which the slaves were forced to survive. I could feel the fire of indignation kindling within him.

"Normally, I discovered later, he jotted everything down in his note-book, taking great care to get every detail right, but on this occasion he was so overcome with horror and sadness that he could not bear to tarry a moment longer on board. Questioning me all the while, he accompanied me to my parents' home.

"But when we reached the house we found they were gone. The neighbours explained that after I had been press-ganged my parents had become so alarmed that the same fate might befall my younger brother – your father, Tom – that they had decided to leave Bristol. They had gone to Cambridge, on the other side of England, and far from the sea. My neighbours gave me their address."

Over the years Uncle Harry stayed in touch with Thomas Clarkson. The university college where he worked, St. John's, was where Clarkson himself had taken his degree. It was here, in 1785, that Clarkson's life was changed when he won first prize in a Latin essay competition on whether it was right to hold slaves. . The idea of holding such a competition was a direct result of the publicity given to what had happened on the *Zong*, which was the subject of a famous trial.

I understood from Uncle Harry that Thomas Clarkson did not know much about slavery until then. He nearly failed to write the essay at all, as he couldn't find material. Then he stumbled on a pamphlet by an American Quaker of French origin, Anthony Benezet, written fifteen years before. Benezet, I later learned, was a gifted and dedicated school-teacher in Philadelphia, who opened a small school for black children in his own home in the evenings, as they would otherwise not have received any education. No doubt, as the Quakers say, he would have seen "that of God" in those eager young faces; and this in turn led him to question the whole system of slavery. How strange, I have often thought, that but for those young schoolchildren the abolition of slavery might have taken a wholly different course.

Clarkson had been intending to become a parish priest, but he could not banish from his mind what he had learned. There was so much that needed to be done. One day, travelling to London, he stopped in Hertfordshire at a place called Wadesmill and dismounted from his horse. Here he spent some time in silent reflection. It came to him that if what he had said in his essay was true, some person would have to put an end to these calamities. Now, he knew, it was his task to be that person.

"Is he the man in the great black cloak I have sometimes seen you talking to in the college?" I inquired of Uncle Harry.

"The very same. He returns to Cambridge from time to time and I also go down to London to hear him speak or to help in other ways. I have never known a man of such energy and determination. For seven years he travelled five thousand miles a year on horseback and by stagecoach, often at night. All over the country he went, but especially to the great slaving ports of Bristol and Liverpool. He corresponded with four hundred people. He gave speeches up and down the land. He questioned ship's captains, ship's doctors and seamen. He built up records on every sailor – and there were five thousand of them – who had sailed in the slave trade, discovering that fully half of them never returned. He wrote pamphlets, reports and whole books on the slave trade. It was precisely such details as I was able to tell him about my journeys that Thomas Clarkson used so tellingly. His was the ammunition that his dear friend William Wilberforce was able to fire off in Parliament with his brilliant speaking gifts. Rarely can there have been such a partnership. Between them they changed the public mood. Until then people didn't know that such terrible things were happening! And behind it all, as the final side of the triangle that was to put an end to the triangle trade, were the Quakers."

Uncle Harry showed me a vast pile of papers containing all the evidence that had been gathered by Thomas Clarkson. There was also a book by him on the history of Quakerism, and another about William Penn and the founding of the state of Pennsylvania in America.

"But is it true that he never became a Quaker, Uncle Harry?"

"He has always remained a member of the Church of England. But you know what he told the Tsar, that he is nine parts Quaker – and we all say the tenth part is more Quakerly than the Quakers!"

"Is that why he has had so much to do with them?"

"Well, you see, the Quakers needed him as much as he needed them. Long before he wrote his essay at Cambridge, Quakers in England and also in America had opposed slavery. They were almost the only ones who did. They carried that torch, but no one took much notice of them. They were on the fringes of society: still now, Quakers cannot be members of Parliament and cannot go to university: you have to be a member of the Church of England. So Quakers have gone into commerce and have had to work behind the scenes. Nine out of the twelve members of the Abolition Committee set up ten years ago were Quakers. They provided Clarkson with the organisation he needed, as well as money, although he put in a great deal of his own too. How, though, were Quakers to speak truth to power? That was where we needed William Wilberforce. It was Thomas Clarkson who did the hard work to find out the vital details we needed. It was a huge job that took up every waking moment of his life and almost cost him his health and indeed life."

I was silent for a moment, and then asked, "Why was what he did so dangerous, Uncle Harry?"

"Why, Tom, he was trying to change the way everyone thought. There were many people who did well out of the system and did not want it to change. Thomas Clarkson was hated by the ship-owners and by the owners of plantations in the West Indies.

"Once, when he was in Liverpool, he went out to the end of a pier on a stormy day. He stood there, watching some rowing boats in the rough seas. Lost in thought at the savage power of the injustice he was fighting, he all at once became aware of a group of men advancing on him. Among them he recognised a slave ship officer and men in the pay of ship-owners, their faces as grey and chiselled as the sea. Realising that in moments he would be pushed into the water, he ran straight at them, his large frame knocking two of them aside, and, fending off their blows, escaped into the streets of the city.

"And it is as well they did not catch him, or perhaps to this day the Quakers would still be the only ones seeking, in vain, to abolish the slave trade."

\* \* \*

It was to take another twenty-six years before slavery itself was abolished in our land. That year, 1833, was a bittersweet one for me, as it was also the year in which both my dear Uncle Harry and William Wilberforce died.

It was, my dear grandchildren, because of Uncle Harry that I myself had become a Quaker, just as he became a Quaker through knowing Thomas Clarkson and coming into contact with Friends. For many years I worked with other Friends to ban slavery altogether. The women were magnificent, demanding abolition straight away, not gradually. Women Friends like Elizabeth Heyrick wrote pamphlets and organised sugar boycotts. Can you imagine that the people in whole towns, like Leicester, stopped putting sugar in their tea because it came from slave-plantations?

In 1840, with Uncle Harry much in mind, I went to the World Anti-Slavery Convention in London, a great occasion attended by over four thousand people. How I wished that Uncle Harry might have heard the eighty-year-old Thomas Clarkson speak! He began by saying that he was the last surviving member of the 1787 Abolition Committee; and ended by saying that the great task now was to banish slavery from the whole world, and especially in America.

If only I could convey to you the simplicity, dignity and feeling with which he spoke. The Quaker women in their bonnets wept and men brushed away tears. When Clarkson sat down there was total stillness in the hall. At length, the chairman rose and thanked us for having paid tribute in silence. Then there was a shout and people leapt to their feet waving hats and handkerchiefs. For several minutes the very building shook, the thunderous applause dying away momentarily only when Thomas Clarkson's nine-year-old grandson Tommy was introduced to the gathering. And then the building shook again with wave upon wave of shouting and wild applause.

I too am growing old, my children, and now it is your task to make sure that this great work is carried forward and that slavery is no more in other parts of the world.

What happened to Thomas Clarkson, you ask? He was to live for a further six years, dying at the age of 86. Although it meant travelling some distance to Ipswich, I knew how much Uncle Harry would have wished me to attend the funeral on his behalf, and so I went.

It was a calm, grey autumn day. The leaves were beginning to turn.

Thomas Clarkson was buried in the churchyard in the village of Playford where he had lived. The occasion was as simple as it could have been, as he himself would have wished. The church was overflowing and the sides of the road from his house to the church were packed with people from far and wide.

Many Friends had come to pay their last respects. You could spot them at a glance from their broad black hats.

As the coffin was led up to the church door, first one, and then all of us, removed our hats.

ON THE SPOT
WHERE STANDS THIS
MONUMENT
IN THE MONTH OF JUNE
1785
THOMAS CLARKSON
RESOLVED
TO DEVOTE HIS LIFE
TO BRINGING ABOUT THE
ABOLITION
OF THE SLAVE
TRADE

# The Fugitive

Mary Brewster was six years old. She loved to get up early and play in a little glade with her imaginary friends. There were not many houses nearby, so they were often the best friends she had.

That particular morning, Nathaniel Brewster was up early too. Mary found him painting the side of the big barn. She loved the old building and often played there too.

"Why are you painting the barn so early in the morning, Grandpa?" asked Mary.

"Well you see Mary dear, if I make an early start I can get this side of the barn painted before the hot sun gets to it. Otherwise the paint might come up in blisters, which we wouldn't want, would we?"

"No," she replied. "Oh, what's all that noise, Grandpa?"

Coming from where they could see the great Ohio River glinting in the early morning sunlight they could hear the sound of shouting, dogs barking and whistles. Her grandfather paused and listened.

"If it weren't so early in the morning I would think it was the slave catchers after someone who has escaped. But you know normally the slaves running away only travel at night."

Mary nodded her head, for sometimes the fugitive slaves would stay at their house. At night they would always have a candle burning in the highest window. When the runaway slaves crossed the Ohio in the dead of night, they would then make their way up the hill to their house. Mary knew that their house was called a "station", because it was on the Underground Railroad: the system of houses and helpers who secretly made it possible for black slaves from the southern states of America to escape and make their way north to Canada.

"Maybe someone had to row across the river at first light," said her grandfather thoughtfully. "I expect the catchers were on to him."

"Will he come here?" Mary inquired.

"He might," said her grandfather.

"What will you do if the catchers come?"

"I don't know, we'll think of something."

Nathaniel was just about to tell her not to stray too far from the house, but she had already gone. As fast as her little feet could take her she scampered off to the glade and quickly summoned all her friends from the invisible places where they lived. She sat down on the ground and told them that a poor man who was usually in chains had managed to get free! "He's come ever such a long way," she explained gravely.

Gathering up her little friends, Mary dashed off through the woods to a large, bare rock from where she could see down over the hillside towards the Ohio. Suddenly, halfway down, she saw a man scrambling up the steep slope for all he was worth. She jumped up and down, waving her arms. At last the man glanced up, caught sight of her and changed direction. He disappeared into some bushes below her just as a group of men on horseback burst into view lower down the slope.

Quickly she dropped down from the rock and went to the path. Within moments, she heard the sound of cracking twigs and panting.

A young black man, almost no more than a boy, appeared below her, his eyes wide with terror. "This way!" she whispered urgently. Grasping a tree root he hauled himself up to where Mary was standing.

"Follow me," she said, "it's a shortcut. They'll have to take the road."

When they got to the barn grandpa was still there, this time with a hammer in his hand. "You run inside, Mary, and tell your mother. Make sure you don't come out."

No more than a few minutes later the posse of slave catchers came pounding up the road, out of breath from the hard ride. They found Nathaniel Brewster calmly hammering up the barn door.

"We know you've got him in there!" shouted the sergeant. "Open up and let us get him!"

Nathaniel calmly kept hammering away.

"Open up or I'll lash you like a dog, you Quaker do-gooder!"

A few more nails went into the door frame.

"Stand aside, Nathaniel Brewster!" roared their leader, who knew the farmer by reputation.

Nathaniel reached down into the pocket of his apron and pulled out another nail.

"Unnail the door!"

"These are round-headed nails," replied Nathaniel evenly. "They take a lot of getting out. In any case, there's nobody in the barn."

"Then why in tarnation are you nailing the door up?"

"We're having trouble with wasps. They always make their nest in the barn. I thought this year I would keep them out."

"Don't play the fool with me Nathaniel Brewster or I'll blow your head off. No man in human history has ever nailed up a barn door to keep out wasps. Did you or didn't you see the runaway slave just now?" The gang leader smiled grimly to himself, for he knew that Quakers set great store by telling the truth.

"I did see the slave, yes."

"Hah, you did! There you are – he's got that no-good Noah Woodson in the barn. Open up in the name of the law!"

"What law?"

"What law? Waddya mean, what law? The Fugitive Slave law of 1850! The new law under which you are required to hand over another man's property."

"If the man is in the barn as you say," replied Nathaniel calmly, "then there's no way he can escape. As you can see, this is the only door and there are no windows, just a few ventilation slits. Your men can guard the building easily. If you want to break down this door under that law, you will need a signed warrant from a magistrate."

There was a stunned silence. The posse put their heads together. Nathaniel could hear the men muttering among themselves.

"He's a man of standing in this community, best be careful."

"He's got the law on his side."

"What's the hurry? He's right – we've got our quarry trapped."

"Ok, ok, you Lewis and the others stay here and keep every side of this barn covered while Ben and I go fetch that warrant." And then, turning to Nathaniel:

"All right, we'll play this by the law, just like we are ourselves law-abiding bounty hunters. There's a good price on the young man's head. Now, Mr Brewster," he went on a bit lamely, "I'd be obliged if you tell me where I can find the nearest magistrate round these here parts."

"I know, Sergeant," said a young man in his posse eagerly, "Mr Anderson's a magistrate. I know where to find him."

Nathaniel did his best not to smile as it became clear that there had been no need for the Sergeant to ask him for help at all. Instead, he said, "Your men are welcome to stay here while you're fetching that warrant. We'll get them some breakfast and coffee, as it may take you some time. It will be at least nine o'clock before Mr Anderson opens up for business, and it's just seven of the morning right now. Could I help you gentlemen to a cup of coffee before you go?"

But the Sergeant, Ben and the young man had already gone. Their horses thundered off down the road towards the small settlement by the Ohio River.

It was eleven o'clock in the morning before they returned. The Sergeant triumphantly waved the warrant. "Open up the barn!"

Nathaniel Brewster carefully examined the warrant. He read it as slowly as he could.

"Everything seems in order," he said to Mary, sticking his brush back into the bucket of paint she had been holding out for him.

With a few deft movements of a crowbar, the round-headed nails came out more easily than expected, with no damage to the timber. The great door swung open. The sun was now playing fully on the front of the barn, and sunlight flooded into the interior. There was a cart, a pile of sacks, various farm implements and some old bales of hay. Nothing else.

"Search the barn," the Sergeant ordered his men. "Remember that the carts often have false bottoms and look for hidden hideouts under the floor."

The cart was all but dismantled. The sacks were lifted up and shaken one by one. Pitchforks were thrust into every single bale of hay. The men banged on the floor with the butts of their rifles to discover any underground chambers. But it soon became clear: the barn was empty.

"You would not believe me," said Nathaniel. "I told you there was nobody in the barn."

"But you said you saw him!"

"I did indeed, but that's not the same as saying that he was inside."

Purple in the face with rage, the Sergeant asked: "Well, if you saw him, which way did he go?"

"I don't know. As you can see, the road divides beyond the farm. You can go left or you go right. I didn't see which way he went."

"Why not?" shouted the Sergeant.

"I had my back to him," explained Nathaniel. "I was painting the barn."

"Which way did you tell him to go?"

"I didn't tell him."

In exasperation the Sergeant swept his men off. Soon there were no more than a few lingering little clouds of dust in the road and the fading sound of horses' footsteps.

"Did you really not tell Noah which way to go?" asked Mary.

"No, Mary, I did not."

"What did you tell him?" she persisted.

"Well, since you ask, I told him that the left-hand fork leads to the next station and that the right-hand fork does not, but that it was up to him to choose and that I did not intend to see which way he went. Besides, it doesn't matter; he's almost half a day ahead of them now. He'll soon be in Canada, a free man."

# The Sheepdog

"Look, mother, here come Mr Edwards and his dog Pip," said Cari excitedly, standing at the window. "I think they're going to the meeting house."

"Oh go on with you Cari Carew," said her mother. "He can't be going to meeting all by himself."

But he was. The old man and his black-and-white sheepdog made their way to the Quaker meeting house next door to the Carews. Mr and Mrs Carew and their eleven-year-old daughter watched them go inside. The great wooden door was left ajar, as though in hope that someone would join them.

"It was strange enough when just the two of them would go, but now that Winifred has died I didn't expect we'd see old Jack any more. It almost makes me think we should go along to keep him company," observed Mr Carew.

"Oh, but dad, it must be so boring!" exclaimed Cari. "Just sitting there in silence for a whole hour and sometimes more. It's bad enough having to go to chapel."

"Now don't you be talking like that, Cari," said her mother sternly.

Her father, though, smiled. "I thought you might quite enjoy seeing Pip lying in the special pen for dogs they have in the meeting house. You've always wanted to have a dog; just think, you could stroke him for the whole hour."

"She would do nothing of the sort," said her mother. "She would sit still like everyone else. In any case, we shan't be going to the meeting house but will stick to our dear chapel."

"How strange," said Cari's father, changing the subject slightly, "to think that just a year or two ago it was such a thriving little meeting. Then the Prices and the Morgans moved away in the space of a few months, and old Meredith Watts died. And now Winifred. I expect Jack is going this one last time to pay his respects to his dearly departed wife and that this will be the end of the Quaker meeting in our village."

But it was not. Week after week, in the snow, in the driving rain and in the bright sunshine, Jack Edwards and Pip would make their way down the narrow, winding main street of the Welsh village to the meeting house each Sunday morning just before the church clock struck eleven. Every Sunday morning, the door would be left ajar; and every Sunday morning the only attenders would be the master and his dog.

Then, one day, Jack died. Quakers from the nearest town came to conduct the funeral service. Jack had been a popular figure in the village and everyone turned out in their black clothes to pay their last respects, dressed if anything more formally than the Quakers themselves, as many of them observed afterwards.

"I suppose the meeting house will be sold now," Mrs Carew said afterwards.

"Aye, that's what the Elders were saying," said her husband. "They're going to keep it on for a little while longer in memory of Jack, but then it will be disposed of."

"What will become of Pip?" asked Cari.

"Jack's neighbours have taken him in. He'll be fine there with the other dogs."

"Oh," said Cari sadly.

It was the Sunday after Jack's funeral. The Carews had been to early morning chapel and were back home again. Shortly before eleven there came a sound of whining and scratching at the door. Mrs Carew went to look.

"Why, whatever next, it's Pip!" she exclaimed. "I expect he just wants to be taken for a walk, like Jack always took him on a Sunday."

"I'll take him!" said Cari eagerly. Her father found an old lead they had hanging on a hook. Cari clipped it onto the dog's collar.

"Off you go! Do you both good to get some exercise," said her mother. "But don't you be too long now."

Dog and daughter returned an hour later. "Wherever have you been?" said Cari's mother crossly. "I told you not to be too long. I was beginning to get worried."

"You will never believe this," said Cari, "but Pip dragged me into the meeting house. That's where he wanted to go. He darted this way and that, as though he was rounding up a sheep, and nipped at my heels until I went in and sat down. Then he wouldn't let me get up again until the clock struck twelve, and here I am!"

Her mother looked astonished. "And you managed to sit there by yourself in silence for a whole hour?"

"Yes, it was quite nice really. I just sat there quietly, surrounded by all the stillness, and didn't even think of stroking Pip, who lay in his pen without making a sound."

Cari couldn't wait to tell her friends Angharad and Jennifer. "If Pip comes again next Sunday, will you come to meeting with me?"

Her friends weren't sure. It sounded very dull to them, but they were intrigued at the idea of the dog that was keeping the meeting going. They agreed to come along the next Sunday morning and see what happened.

The next Sunday, just before eleven, Pip scratched at their door. Cari went out into the street, as did her mother and father, who also wanted to see what the dog did. Angharad and Jennifer were there, giggling and laughing. "Look, he's rounding Cari up!"

The dog barked at the two girls too and began herding them towards the meeting house door. Mrs Carew said "Well I never," and was just about to close her own door when the dog rushed up the steps and blocked her passage, barking and growling.

"I do believe that dog wants us to go to meeting as well," declared Mr Carew. "Come on, Mrs Carew, in memory of Jack." And they joined the others.

The dog ushered his little flock into the meeting house. Mr Carew carefully left the door ajar. They all sat down in a circle. Pip went over to his pen.

After a few minutes Mrs Carew grew bored and restive. She remembered all the things she had to do and got to her feet and began to tip-
toe out of the room. A black-and-white blur arrived at the door before
she could reach the street. Pip growled softly but menacingly. Startled,
Mrs Carew backed away and sat down again. Soundlessly, but still
keeping a keen eye on everyone, Pip returned to the pen. When the
clock struck twelve Pip calmly went over to the door to be let out.
Meeting was over.

The next week, in their grocery shop, Mr and Mrs Carew found
themselves quizzed about the meeting by what seemed the whole
village.

"It was strange," said Mrs Carew. "After a while I settled down and it
was almost as though I could sense Jack there in spirit, and all the others who used to attend. Why, I even found myself on my feet at one

point saying how the stillness touched my very soul. There's no reason why you can't go to both chapel and Quaker meeting. I think I shall keep going."

The next Sunday morning the same five people were present, although this time they went straight to the meeting house and Pip didn't have to round them up. He did, however, find other interested onlookers in the street and, dashing this way and that, and barking here and growling there, he gathered up his flock, some willing and others less so, making it impossible for them to do anything but enter the meeting room and sit down.

This time there was a good-sized meeting and several people, much to their surprise, found themselves on their feet, talking about gentleness, honesty and simplicity, about the unseen presence in their midst and about how animals sometimes knew things that people didn't.

Week after week the meeting grew. Pip no longer needed to drive people into the meeting house but would greet them at the door, tail going to and fro. People from neighbouring villages came too: at first out of curiosity, and then out of conviction. A children's class was set up for Cari and her friends. Elders were appointed, and a clerk.

The meeting house was never sold.

# A Black Bible and a White Carnation

"They're moving out of Bridge Street," he said late one day, putting down his cap and coat.

"Who are?" she said, as she hung them up.

"Why, Cadbury's of course."

"Whatever do you mean, John Dean, 'Cadbury's of course'?"

"Just that, lass; they're moving the whole caboodle four miles out of town."

"Caboodle indeed. You do come back from work with some fine words!"

"Well, that's how it is: the whole Works are being moved lock stock and barrel out beyond Selly Oak."

"Why, but that's just farmland."

"Aye, it is, but soon there will be a cocoa factory there. We've become too cramped where we are now."

"Well, I suppose you'll have to catch the train."

"It's only four or so miles. I thought I might walk."

"The exercise would do you good. Get rid of some of that beer belly."

"Beer belly? What beer belly, lass? You just put my supper on the table and then I'm off to the pub to share the news with Henry."

It was 1879. John had only recently started at Cadbury's. It had been a good job to land, especially as John lacked any skills. The chocolate factory would be expanding even more rapidly with the move to the new site, and there was every prospect of progressing if only he could get training. Advancement would be welcome, as their first baby was on the way.

Henry was John's great friend. John and Henry had grown up in the same street, had gone to the same school, and had both gone out to work at the age of twelve. They used to go fishing together and had played football in the park and in the street with a ball made of rags tied tightly together. When they reached the age of eighteen they started going to the pub together, like so many of the other men living in the mean backstreets of Birmingham.

John knew that Henry wanted to work for Cadbury's, and thought he would be interested in the news. Henry, however, was staring morosely into his glass of dark ale.

"What's up?" said John.

"Lost me job, haven't I," said Henry without looking up. Like John, he had recently found a good job, in his case with the Great Western Railway. Until then, both of them had had a succession of poorly paid and labouring jobs since leaving school at the age of 12.

"Why?" was all that John could find to say.

"Turned up late for work again."

"They did warn you," said John. "Look, I've been trying to spend less time in the pub, what with a new wife and now a baby on the way, and perhaps you should too."

"It wasn't just that. I got into another fight as well," he said, glancing up.

"I'm really sorry about that, Henry," said John. "But – I've got what could be good news. Cadbury's are moving from Bridge Street to the Bournbrook Estate."

"Bournbrook Estate? Never heard of it."

"South of here, in the countryside. You know, around the Bourn, where we used to go trout fishing. The company is expanding and needs more space and are sure to be recruiting new people. I could put in a good word for you."

"I don't need your charity," Henry said bitterly.

"Funny you should say charity," mused John, trying to change the subject. "That was one of the words Mr Cadbury used at morning service earlier in the week. He always says a few words after a Bible reading and silence for prayer, and what he says can really make you think. This time he spoke about 'faith, hope and charity'. I think it's in the Bible somewhere. I'd never realised that 'charity' also meant love or concern for others, had you?"

"Don't you go all religious on me now, John Dean," said Henry truculently. "Religion's all right for all those pious types in their smart suits but none of the folks around here ever set foot inside a church unless they have to."

The more he drank, the more aggressive he became, until as the evening wore on he almost got into a fight with some of the other regulars.

Pushing, pulling and pleading, John succeeded in getting Henry out of the Swan with Two Necks and into the street. The fresh air – if that was what one could call the grime-laden atmosphere of industrial Birmingham – hit them like a wall.

"You can't go back in, Henry," said John. "You've lost your job, you've got no money, and besides ..."

He hesitated. He could see that far from sobering Henry up, the damp cold appeared to enrage him.

"Besides what?" Henry snapped. "That you can't take your liquor?"

"Come on, Henry, it's not a competition. I'm just trying to tell you what's for your own good. You're on the way to letting drink get the better of you."

John barely saw the fist coming but just managed to jerk his head out of the way. Something in him snapped, and he swung back. Next thing the two of them were rolling on the pavement and in the gutter. The thin, shrill sound of a policeman's whistle pierced the night air. In an instant they stopped, scrambled to their feet and made off into the misty night.

Mary was still up when he got back. She flung her arms around him but then stepped back in dismay. "Whatever's happened? Your face cut and swollen, reeking of drink and smoke and your clothes all dirty and torn. It's that Henry Bowker, I know it is, he's no good for you that man isn't!"

Controlling her exasperation, she swabbed his face down with a wet cloth. "If you're not careful, John Dean," she said, "they'll be showing you the door at Cadbury's just like Great Western sent Henry packing. You should keep away from him."

"He's my best friend," said John. "I've known him all my life. I can't just abandon him."

"That man will sink a whole lot lower before he starts pulling himself together," Mary declared. "You just count your blessings that you've got a good job and don't you go messing things up like so many of the men around here. You're a good man, kind and decent, although you don't deserve me telling you that right now. Stay away from him and the others, I tell you."

By morning the bruising was showing but John decided to go to work as normal, hoping that nobody would notice anything. His job was to load the sacks of cocoa beans onto the runner taking them to the top of the Cocoa Stack. He did not mind the physical labour, though even now, after just a few months in the job, he was beginning to find the repetitive work a bit monotonous. But he could barely read and write, and so there were limits to what he was able to do.

That particular day, though, his mind was full of thoughts of the evening before and what might become of his friend, and also of the baby that was on the way. Here he was, in his first job with real prospects, while Henry – well, what kind of future awaited Henry? The army? Prison?

John was far away in thought when he became aware of his supervisor standing by his side. "Mr Cadbury would like to have a word with you," he said.

Snapping back to reality, John found himself before the stocky, bearded figure of George Cadbury. He was a distinguished looking man whose face combined great strength of character with kindliness. John had met him when he first joined the firm, but they had not spoken since. George Cadbury asked him how he was liking the work. Seemingly reading John's mind, he asked whether he did not find the endless stacking of sacks boring.

"I suppose it is, sir," John replied, "but I have my thoughts to keep me company, and there are always new ways of doing things."

"Yes," said his supervisor, Mr Cooper, "John has already come up with a new method of stacking the bags, which works very well."

George Cadbury questioned him closely about the changes he had made. Just as he was leaving, he said, "Nasty bruises, those, on your face, John. Have them seen to by the medical service."

John protested feebly that there was nothing the matter. George Cadbury fell silent, and John knew that he should say something by way of explanation. He knew that George Cadbury disapproved of drinking – but also that he set great store by telling the truth, as John himself did.

"You can probably guess, sir, where I was. I am ashamed to say that I got into a scrap – with my best friend, in fact. He'd just lost his job with the railways."

George Cadbury shot him a searching look. John felt that all his weaknesses and limitations were laid bare, not thinking for a moment that what the owner of the factory might also be seeing were honesty, intelligence and loyalty.

Some days later, Mr Cooper came up to him. "Mr Cadbury would like to see you in his study. I don't know what it's about."

John reluctantly made his way to the study. Perhaps Mr Cadbury had decided to show him the door, as Mary had said.

"Ah, John, thank you for coming. I have been thinking about what Mr Cooper said and how you have been coming up with imaginative ideas. You are a bright young man and with training could go far. But you'd need to be able to read and write properly. What I would like to suggest is that you begin attending the Adult School. You may know that I've been taking a class there for the last ten years or so."

John knew about the school. It took men in off the streets on Sunday mornings, teaching them to read and write and giving instruction in the Scriptures. Some of those who went came from good homes but others were from the worst of the slums; some, he had heard, were even ex-prisoners. It would mean giving up his precious Sunday mornings, and although Mr Cadbury's words at morning service often impressed him, he did not much fancy studying the Bible; he knew too that many of those who attended the Adult School gave up drinking.

"I know how much difference the classes can make to people's lives," said John slowly. "I have seen that myself, although not everyone's in favour. Can I think about your suggestion, sir, and let you know in a day or two?"

"Of course," George Cadbury replied. "Discuss it with others, like your friend whom you mentioned, and with Mrs Dean."

Not many men consulted their wives on major decisions of this kind, and John was struck by the remark.

"I will, sir. And – as for my friend Henry Bowker: if I might be so bold, is there any chance that he could get a job at the Works?"

"There is every chance, but I suggest that he come along to the Adult School first too. I have seen many men brought out of the darkness into God's marvellous light. Men, I am fond of saying, are saved to serve! But first he needs to feel part of our great family."

That evening John told Mary all about it. As he expected, she brushed his objections aside. "He's right: it's your one chance to get ahead," she said emphatically. "Don't worry about some of the other type of people who attend. They're like Henry – people who are their own worst enemies but nevertheless have a lot of good in them."

" 'That of God in everyone', Mr Cadbury calls it. He always sees the best in people."

"And he does in you too, John. And now that Cadbury's have stopped Saturday afternoon working it won't be half so bad missing your lie-in of a Sunday morning!"

Back at the Swan with Two Necks, friendship re-established and the fight all but forgotten, Henry saw matters very differently.

"Go back to school? Whatever for? What good did school do us? You're not earning bad money: just you be satisfied with that, John Dean, and don't you start getting ideas above your station."

"But Henry, I'm not just talking about me. Mr Cadbury was also asking whether you'd come along. If you did, it might open the way for you to join Cadbury's."

"And to give up the public house and start reading the Bible and seeing the light: no thank you very much. I've heard stories about that George Cadbury, and besides I've got a job with a builder now."

In vain did John argue with him. He knew he was touching on very sensitive areas and had to tread carefully. The builder had a bad reputation, like many others in the trade; they were simply out to make quick money. By contrast George Cadbury was, John knew, trying to improve not just education and ways of thinking but people's circumstances; how, as he put it, could a man cultivate ideals when his home was a slum and his only possible place of recreation the public house? John was beginning to see all this, but it was not something he could discuss with his friend.

Going along to the Adult School in Bristol Street for the first time, John was astonished to find that there were some three hundred men there. George Cadbury seemed to know each and every one by name.

John took great advantage of the lessons, progressing rapidly. Although George Cadbury never offered anyone privileges for attending the Adult School, the progress John made meant that he was now able to read manuals and undertake special training. After a few years he became an expert fitter and worked on the chocolate-making machines – the refiners with the five rollers, the conching machines for kneading the liquid chocolate, and the spinners for making Easter eggs. The advancement at work was just as well, for he and Mary now had three children: Harry, Billy and Maggie.

What with the extra responsibilities John no longer met Henry in the pub. There was however also another reason: John was beginning to take to heart the different way of life that the Adult School had opened up for him. He would often call to mind the time that George had spoken about St Francis's love of animals and understanding for them. "The cat," he had said, "would be the first person in the house to know if the man had 'become a Christian'. It was the cat who would know whether a man had put away the drink, given up gambling and could govern his temper."

John and Henry did however have another tie. In 1881 Henry too had got married and he and his wife Ruth had a son, Matthew, who was the same age as their daughter Maggie. Matthew and Maggie often played together.

His job with the builder had lasted just over a year. The builder had gone bankrupt, and Henry now had a job as a coal man. Even though he had a strong back and was not averse to exercise, he disliked the work, which was poorly paid.

One day, Matthew and Maggie were playing on the living room floor. John had made some simple blocks, which Henry had painted in bright reds, yellows and blues. They were pleased to see how eagerly the children took to them. Matthew and Maggie built a little tower, in the middle of which they placed a white flower which Mary had given them. Henry observed, "Just look at them playing, like a little man and wife they are. Soon they'll be going to school; just think, you have to now, it's the law. You and I were lucky to get any schooling at all."

He paused. "And now you're even a teacher at the Adult School. I've been thinking of late about what you said that I should come along too. It's just that – well, I'm worried that I might be a bit old."

"Old? Why, you're not even thirty! Many of the men who start are much older than that."

"It's not just that. It's – it's that I don't like all this preaching George Cadbury goes in for and all the things I know I would have to live up to."

"It's not really like that, Henry. Mr Cadbury knows who you are and would welcome you warmly. He doesn't really preach *at* us. He's kindly and makes us think. It's hard to describe, but we're like a big group of friends."

Despite his misgivings, Henry decided to give the Adult School a try. He soon turned out to be one of the brighter members of the class. To begin with there would still be the odd time when he failed to appear, but before long he had become a stalwart member of the group. On many a Sunday morning he would join John and others and venture into the worst parts of Birmingham in the early hours of the morning to find people who had failed to appear. Some would still be drunk from the night before, or be too ashamed of the poor clothes they wore; no matter, they would still be persuaded to attend, and Henry would always notice how George Cadbury's eyes would light up as these men walked through the door.

There had, however, also been one other thing that had tipped the scales for Henry when deciding to attend. It was a small thing: a flower. It was George Cadbury's custom of handing out a flower at the end of every class to all those present. He himself always wore a flower in his buttonhole, and took a special delight in sending each man away with one, which they could select from the huge cardboard box of blooms he brought along. John had told him of the first time he had come home with a flower when he first started going to the Adult School several years before.

"I've brought this home, lass," John said, handing her the carnation sheepishly. "It's a gift from Mr Cadbury."

Mary looked at the white flower in amazement. Silently she placed it in a vase and stood it in pride of place on the mantelpiece. The flower seemed to fill the drab room with light.

"What is it, Mary?" he said, seeing how moved she was.

"Why, it lights up the whole room, that one flower does. It's just so beautiful – otherwise all I ever see is brick, brick, brick."

Harry, Billy and Maggie even when small also loved it when their father returned home from the class bearing a flower. Sometimes it would be a rose, sometimes a dahlia, sometimes a carnation. Mr Cadbury always let him choose and whenever he could John would select a white bloom. Mostly it would stand in the vase on the mantelpiece, but other times it would find its way onto the floor for the children to play with. And now Henry too would be bringing back a bloom.

Some years after he had begun attending the Adult School, Henry told John that, more than anything else, it had been the story about the the flower that had persuaded him to think again about attending the the Adult School.

The Sunday after Henry had mentioned this, John murmured to Mr Cadbury as he was selecting his flower: "You'd be surprised, sir, if you saw what happened to these. When I get back the children are always waiting for me at the corner to see what I've brought home. You should hear them shrieking and laughing as they wave it about and run inside to show their mother. It's the highlight of their week."

"John, I'm so very glad you have told me. It does my heart good to know that. I do believe that the love of flowers leads to the love of all natural and wholesome things."

"And is not just my children that love them, but their friends too, like young Matthew, Henry's son."

"Henry is doing well," observed George Cadbury slowly, "he seems a changed man."

"That he is indeed," replied John. "It may not be my place to say so, sir, but, well, if you were ever looking for someone at the Works, I'm sure he's your man."

The two men both smiled inwardly: John because he had at last managed to tell George Cadbury what he had long been wanting to say, and George Cadbury because he had confirmed what he had long suspected.

It was shortly afterwards that that a job came up at Cadbury's and that Henry, after not much persuasion by John, applied. He was accepted.

\*    \*    \*

Eight years later, in 1893, John returned home late one afternoon from work.

"Remember how they moved the Works out to Bournbrook thirteen years ago? Well, now George Cadbury wants to build a whole new village, to be called Bournville, with housing for the workforce. We could move out of Birmingham to the countryside."

Mary looked pleased, but also paused. "What about me mam and Jessica next door and Auntie Agnes and Uncle Bob around the corner?" she said reflectively. "And then there's the local shops, and the children and their school and friends and Henry and Ruth and little Matthew in the next street. I'm just not sure, John."

"Well, Henry and Ruth might decide to move as well. In any case, we don't have to decide today. There's a meeting planned for next week when it's all going to be explained."

And so it was that John and Mary Dean walked to the station to catch the train to the Cadbury plant one misty autumn evening. Fog played around the gas streetlights; the sharp, sweet smell of coal hung in the air.

After a Bible reading, prayer and short Quaker silence, George Cadbury spoke from the lectern. Moving the Works had been a success. Now it would be possible to move home as well. It was all very well to have ideals, but these could only be put into effect if people lived in better conditions. They would be exchanging the grime, smoke and bustle of central Birmingham for the spacious, clean surroundings near the Works – the "factory in the garden", as it was known. People working for Cadbury's did not have to move but if they did want to, a house would be available for them. It would be for rent, but the rent would gradually pay off the house. Each house would have its own garden; in fact the house could occupy no more than a quarter of the land. They would be spacious and well fitted out. There would be wide roads, local schools, playgrounds, parks, health facilities and playing fields.

Plans of the Bournville area and the individual houses were on display. After the talk John and Mary pored over the plans and the scale-model houses. "Each house looks different," she said wonderingly. "All set back from the road, and not in long straight rows."

George Cadbury came out to meet them. "Do you like what you see, Mary?"

"I was reluctant to begin with," Mary said shyly. "It would mean leaving friends and family behind and everything we know. But I didn't realise it was all going to be so – so nice-looking."

"It's important that everyone should be housed well. How else can we do our work properly if we are not? You would soon settle in and get used to the change." George Cadbury moved on.

"How did he know my name?" Mary whispered to John when George was out of earshot.

"He knows everyone's name," replied John. "Sometimes I think we are more like one big family for Mr Cadbury than workers. He treats us all like equals – although I haven't yet dare call him George!"

John and Mary did their sums. They found that for very little more rent than they were paying in Birmingham they could have a house that would become their own after just twelve years. Why, that was little more than Maggie's age, and how those years had flown by!

They decided to take the plunge. Now, each morning, instead of running to catch the train (for he had long since stopped making the long walk to work), John would wait until the Bull sounded – the steam hooter that went off every morning ten minutes before work started at a quarter to eight. Strolling down Linden Road he would reach the new factory comfortably on time, surrounded by the hundreds of people coming from Birmingham on foot or arriving by train.

It was true that Maggie might no longer be able to chalk out her squares for hopscotch in the street, but then, as her mother said, "She's getting a bit old for that; regular little lady, she is now!" Harry and Billy played cricket in the garden instead, while their father tended the vegetable patch. "Mind the young fruit trees!" he would shout to the boys. He and Mary never managed to get over the fact that apple, plum and cherry trees had already been planted in the garden before

they arrived. "It's enough to make the move without having to start a garden from scratch," George Cadbury was heard to say.

To John and Mary's delight, Henry and Ruth also decided to move to Bournville. Once again they were in the next street, and once again their children were able to play together.

Several years went by. It almost went without saying that when Maggie started work she would follow her two elder brothers and join Cadbury's. Like the others she would arrive in her smart clothes and hat and then change into a clean white uniform. She worked in the marzipan room, and later also in the chocolate packing room, sitting at the bench on one of the special high stools. The conditions were light and airy, and it was possible to chat. Nearly all the others were young like herself, as married women had to stop work; a woman's place was in the home and it was not considered right for a woman to combine a family with employment.

From time to time Maggie would meet Mr Cadbury. He knew her by name, and would always stop to talk briefly, asking after her family and how she was getting on at work.

Like father, like son: Matthew also joined his father at Cadbury's.

He was assigned to the Maintenance Department, of which John was now head. It turned out that Matthew was interested in growing flowers and vegetables even though he knew nothing about gardening, and he made regular visits to the Deans' home and garden.

At the same time, he always managed to exchange a few words with Maggie on arriving or leaving, or if possible both. Before long, these meetings were taking longer than the horticultural instructions at the bottom of the garden, and it came as no surprise when they decided to get married.

It was the custom for a woman newly engaged to visit Mr Cadbury in his study. She would be given a Bible as a parting gift for when she got married and had to leave work.

Maggie duly knocked on the door and went in. Any nervousness she had been feeling disappeared in the warmth and kindness with which she was received. "We shall be sorry to lose you, Maggie," George Cadbury said. "I have heard nothing but good about you – but then that is only what I would have expected, knowing your father."

Maggie stammered a few words of thanks and then, not quite knowing what to say, exclaimed, "Oh, what a beautiful white carnation you have in your buttonhole!"

"Do you like it?" he asked. "I do so like their delicate scent."

"It's a lovely one," she said. "They're one of the flowers that Father grows. I remember he would sometimes bring home a carnation from the Adult School."

"I know!" replied George Cadbury. "He told me how you would welcome him when he returned home and rush in with the flower to show your mother."

Taking the carnation from his buttonhole he placed it gently on the black Bible. "I should like you to have it," he said. "This time you can be the one to take a flower home."

From that day on, it became a tradition for every young woman who left upon becoming engaged to be given not just a Bible by George Cadbury, but also a carnation.

# The Enemy Within

"Jim, I don't think you should do this. It's just not right."

"You leave that for me to decide, woman," came the angry reply. "There's no need for you to get involved."

"But there is," Ethel Wilson said, softly but insistently, "there's no need to march on Dr Salter's house. I know what you men are like, the next thing you'll be throwing bricks through his windows. Look at you, all dressed up in black and with a cap pulled down right over your head so they won't be able to see your face."

Her husband grew even angrier. "A lot of young men from Bermondsey have already died in this war. If it goes on much longer people of my age might even be called up. It's a disgrace that the doctor won't have us fight the Germans."

"You men are all the same," said Ethel Wilson. "It's men who started this war, and men who want to fight it – just like you want to storm Dr Salter's house. And why him, of all people; have you forgotten what he did for Jennifer?"

Her husband paused. Their neighbours' daughter had nearly died of diphtheria three years before. "I know," he said, shifting his weight uncomfortably to the other foot.

"He even stayed there the night," said his wife. "Wouldn't leave Jennifer's side till he knew she was out of danger. We've never had a doctor like him in this part of London. People spill out onto the pavement waiting their turn to see him. Before the war we all thought he was a saint. And now, all because he won't support this senseless killing, you turn on him."

"You're just as bad as all those pacifists," said Jim. "Lily-livered cowards betraying king and country, that's what they are."

"They're nothing of the sort," his wife retorted. "If everyone thought like Dr Salter there would be no wars. But even if you disagree with him, remember Jennifer."

"I know, I know, he didn't even charge the Browns because he knew they couldn't afford it. Every time I see Jennifer I remember what he did. But even great men can get things wrong. The men are very angry about what happened at the Institute."

Two days earlier a group of soldiers, sailors and dockers had emerged from the pub and marched on the Institute of the Independent Labour Party, an organisation that was firmly against the war. Word got about that action was being planned. Arthur Gillian, a tough, powerfully built man who opposed the war but was also known for his short fuse and hard fists, joined up with the Institute caretaker. Together they locked all the doors and windows and barricaded up the front door with benches in such a way that anyone entering the building would have to do so one at a time.

Rocks were thrown, the door was rammed and splintered, and eventually a passageway was forced into the building. As the men pushed their way through the barricade, half crawling, Arthur Gillian was waiting for them with an iron rod. One after another the men were laid out. Some were left bleeding and others unconscious. By the time the police arrived on the scene, Gillian's fists were red and raw.

However much Dr Salter was respected, especially for all he had done so selflessly for the community in Bermondsey, he was the director of the Institute and it was decided that he would have to be made an example of. But soon there was talk going round of what had happened after the raid.

"You know as well as I do that people say they have never seen Dr Salter so angry. Tore a right strip off Arthur Gillian when he got there at three in the morning, the doctor did. Said he was ashamed Gillian had used violence and betrayed everything they stood for. Dr Salter is not responsible for what Gillian did. To attack his home is revenge gone mad."

But there was no persuading her husband. Not to have joined his mates would have meant unthinkable loss of face. Mumbling "I have no choice, but I'll see what I can do," he stumbled out of the house.

Jim Wilson joined the others as arranged at the public house. Late in the evening the knot of men advanced on Dr Salter's home in Storks Road. Some had been drinking heavily and were fired up, some were angry, others were sullen and silent.

"Strange business this," Jim said to two of his companions as they walked along Jamaica Road. "They say he was the most brilliant young doctor in the country. Won every prize, he did, and then turned it all up to come and work here in Bermondsey."

"That's as may be," said one of the others evenly. "But you makes your bed and you've got to lie on it."

"That's right, we're at war: you're either for us or you're agin us," said the other.

"He can also put people's backs up," said the first man. "Very blunt and outspoken, he can be."

"Maybe," said Jim glancing around, "but there's hardly anyone here who hasn't benefited from this man and his dedication to our community."

The men marched raggedly through the dockland streets. Around him he caught snatches of conversation.

"He's one of us, this isn't right. He treats us all as equals."

"That right, he sent his daughter Joyce to our own school, where she probably caught the scarlet fever that killed her. Just eight years of age, she was."

"He's a Quaker and simply acting on his beliefs. They've always been pacifists."

"But the Bible tells us to fight the good fight and carry a sword too."

"'Thou shalt not kill', Salter's always quoting."

"Yes, but what when a country raises a huge army and starts attacking us? Do we stand by idly?"

"If he were a fighting man he could deal with them single-handedly – he's got more energy than anyone I know! He can put the fear of God into anybody, can that man."

They were drawing close to 5 Storks Road now. There were men who had volunteered to serve, there were dockers, there were factory workers. The air was heavy with acrid smoke and the sweet smell of brewing, biscuit factories and glue. The encircling gloom matched the mood of many of the men.

As they turned the final corner into Storks Road, Jim's thoughts went back to the conversation with his wife. Were they really to turn on this man? He thought too of what he had heard one of the men say about Salter's daughter Joyce. She had been adored in Bermondsey. They called her "a little ray of sunshine". When it was known that her life was in danger, people massed in the road outside Ada and Alf Salter's house waiting for news. Jim was among them. They waited until midnight, when the dreaded announcement came that Joyce had died.

Now too it was late in the evening and soon he would be standing in front of the same house. Jim felt the growing tension among the men. They were silent now, and almost resigned to doing something against their own deepest will. Most would probably just have made their point by standing outside the house in silent protest. But there were also a few hotheads among them, and some were outsiders who knew nothing of Salter while others had already lost sons or brothers in the war.

They reached the house. The lights were still on; Salter always worked late on local council and professional paperwork once the work of the day with his patients was done. The band of men stood before the house uncertainly. In the silence the doubts of those like Jim communicated themselves to the militants, while those wanting peaceful protest were acutely aware of the pent-up tension in favour of action.

Perhaps they would have just stood there and eventually melted away; perhaps someone would have knocked on the door and spoken for them all; perhaps there would have been a shout and some chanting and they would have drifted off into the dark, grey fog. But one of the men stumbled over a loose piece of brick lying in the road. Swearing, he picked it up and hurled it at the house shouting, "Take that, you stooge of the enemy!" The tension broke and in an instant others were picking up bricks and emptying their pockets of the stones they had brought along. A barrage of missiles descended on the house.

A window-box was wrenched off the wall and dashed to the ground. An almost palpable shockwave ran through the crowd, many of whom knew the Salters' determination to bring beauty and colour to the drabness of Bermondsey – and that, in tribute to Joyce, the yard behind the house had been turned with all sorts of creepers and climbing plants into what was known as the Green Parlour.

The window box clattered to the ground, scattering its contents over the pavement. The salvo of missiles stopped. Just at that point, the front door swung open. Stones in hand, the men stood there as Dr Salter emerged. His high-domed, bald head gleamed in the soft light. His pince-nez spectacles quivered on his nose, but otherwise he stood in the doorway with total calmness.

Salter's eyes swept the crowd like a lighthouse beacon. Some of the men returned his gaze but others looked away. The doctor stood there,

as inviting a target as one could wish.

"What is this, my friends?" he asked. "Are we to practise violence on those who refuse to visit it on others? Ask yourselves: would Jesus thrust his bayonet into the body of a German workman? There can only be one answer.

"I've looked after you when you were sick. I've served you night and day. Is this the way you reward me? Go home and be ashamed of yourselves!"

The doctor remained in the doorway, catching the eye of every man who would look at him. Then he turned and went back inside, pulling the door to calmly behind him.

The words had gone through the men like a lash. For a moment, it was unclear how they would react. Rage and shame rippled through the crowd in equal measure. Jim caught himself trembling from head to foot. Then, without quite knowing why, he slipped off into the night. A little knot of men followed him, and then a few more. Not a word was spoken. Now everyone was shuffling away. Not a soul dared look back at the house. The night swallowed them up as they went their separate ways.

# The Charge

The bell tinkled as the young man entered the barbershop. There was no one else waiting and the barber motioned to him to sit down in the large black swivel chair. Thomas Evans walked across the faded, curling linoleum with a noticeable limp.

Putting down his cigarette, the barber tucked a gown around Thomas's neck. "War wound?" he said, with a slight nod in the direction of the young man's leg.

Thomas was used to the question, but still didn't know how best to answer it. Although the war had been over for four months, his limp was often still the first topic of conversation.

"No, not exactly," he replied. "Due to the war, you might say, but not a war wound as such."

"Ah," said the barber, as he began snipping away. "In the war effort, then."

"Well, no, I couldn't say that," replied Thomas hesitantly.

The barber put down the comb he had been holding in his left hand, picked up the cigarette again and inhaled deeply. "You couldn't say that?" he asked.

"Look, do you mind if we leave the subject of my wound to one side?"

There was a silence. The balding barber stubbed out the cigarette. Snip-snip, snip-snip went the scissors. Then he paused.

"I lost a son in the war. Are you telling me you were a conchie?"

The world began to spin before Thomas's eyes. "I'm sorry about your son. Yes, I was a conscientious objector."

The barber stopped snipping. "Well," he said slowly, removing the gown, "in that case I have a conscientious objection towards cutting your hair."

Thomas remained seated for a moment, trying to take in what the man had said. Then he got up and stumbled towards the hatstand for his coat, which he pulled on, and hastily flung his scarf around his neck.

*It's nothing to be ashamed of,* he said to himself in the street. *It's just so very hard that people are always down on me without knowing anything about my story.*

Catching his reflection in a shop window he could see that he looked oddly lopsided, with the hair neatly clipped short on one side of his head but still long on the other. Some distance down the road he came across another barbershop. The chair was empty. He decided to go in.

"Hullo, what have we got here?" the barber asked. "Job half done? Mice been getting at you in the night?"

Thomas was weary at having constantly to cover up for his beliefs. He decided to come clean right from the start. "Your colleague up the road refused to continue when he learnt that I'd been a conscientious objector."

"Did he now. Well, I better charge you half price! Mind you, second half mightn't be as good as the first."

"You don't mean to turn me away?" asked Thomas.

"I mightn't agree with your stand, but I admire your courage in coming straight out with the reason for that mangled haircut. Not many people would do that. I bet you have quite a story to tell."

"Yes," said Thomas quietly, more to himself than to the barber, "I do have quite a story to tell."

It was the end of the day. Outside the light was fading. The barber walked over to the door and turned round the sign to read "Closed".

"Tell me as much or as little as you want," he said. "I'll make us both a cup of tea."

\* \* \*

I'd always been against war. Even as a child I thought it was the most ridiculous way to settle disputes. Oh, don't get me wrong, I used to play soldiers like any small boy, but always in the back of my mind I would be thinking how strange it was that we could want to kill other people we didn't even know.

In fact, I felt so strongly about this that it was one of the main reasons I became a Quaker. Don't know much about them, you say? No, neither did I. I just knew that they were against violence and war. When the war came, in 1914, and nearly all my friends volunteered to join the armed forces, it felt strange. There they all were, so excited and patriotic and all eagerly wanting me to sign up too. But I wouldn't, or couldn't. It was hard.

One evening I went to an anti-war meeting. It was held in London, at the Friends meeting house in Bishopsgate. There was an angry crowd in the street of soldiers and others – almost a riot, really. The chairman said that rather than applauding the speakers, which could be heard outside the building, we should wave our handkerchiefs. That was how we voted too, by holding up our handkerchiefs. A number of Quakers spoke out against war, and I was able to talk to some of them afterwards. The relief was more than I can put into words. Here, at last, were other people who felt the same as I did and who, moreover, were able to back up their beliefs with all sorts of arguments, especially from the teachings of Jesus.

Even though so many people flocked to join up when it was voluntary, it was obvious that the government would soon introduce conscription and force people to join the army. I thought that the government had no such right over people's lives.

By this time I was a Quaker and I decided to join the Friends Ambulance Unit, which had been set up at the start of the war. I underwent some training and joined the unit in France. Because I was a chemist, they put me to work in a hospital. Well, a hospital in name only. It consisted of two dimly lit sheds, with hundreds of wounded packed in like sardines. It was almost impossible to walk between them. People were moaning and crying, some screaming all night. The injuries were worse than one can imagine. People were dying, while others were being brought in. All we had was one French medical student and two English officers and us volunteers. Our job was to load the wounded onto the hospital ships. The misery and pain will haunt me for the rest of my days. We worked day and night, snatching no more than a few hours sleep now and then.

Later things got slightly better and, since I could speak some French, I was sent out to make purchases in a French town. Here I was able to talk to people and tell them how I hated war. Most people were astonished – except the mothers, who understood straight away what I meant.

Later again the Friends Ambulance Unit worked close to the Front where the fighting was worst. Day and night we loaded up the wounded who were still able to travel and took them to the nearest railway

# The Charge

station, giving them cocoa, chocolate and biscuits. They came in on stretchers, often choking and gasping. I noticed that the French doctors and stretcher bearers drew no distinction between our own soldiers and German soldiers. I didn't either – we were all creatures of God caught up in this ghastly hell. We worked under terrible pressure, often not eating, washing or sleeping properly for several days on end.

When we first went out we thought the war would be over in a few months. We thought we'd be sharing in the cause of Peace. Instead I found out that living for peace took even more courage than dying for a cause. It was so hard to cling on to a spiritual life; there was so much horror and madness. I'd gone out with a sense of joy and real purpose. Now, after seeing so many young people smashed up and killed, all that was gone. I was troubled whether I was also helping the war effort by aiding the wounded. What we were doing would still be done if we were not there, but by regular soldiers. And of course before our very eyes we saw people who were prepared to die for a cause. This was the greatest sacrifice: not to share with them in surrendering everything. Mine too was a self-surrender, of a spiritual kind, but many times the distinction between what I was doing and what they were doing became blurred. We were all caught up in this together, but doing different things. I felt part of them, and they part of me. Strange though it may sound, there was a sense of closeness and communion in those times of extreme danger and sacrifice that reminded me of the sense of connection you find in a Quaker meeting. All we do then, you see, is to sit together in silence, sharing in the Spirit, which can be every bit as intense and deep as what we found on the Front.

The thought of those who'd stayed at home in England in the cause of peace was also constantly on my mind. We would receive written accounts of the stand they were taking. We knew that some were holding out against the authorities and were even being imprisoned. They were involved in a struggle every bit as much as we were. They were living out their total opposition to military service, and that was compulsory by now. War was a denial of human brotherhood, and they said it could be banished only if people were true to their principles. I was no longer sure I was doing that in France. I decided I had to return.

I tried to obtain work at the laboratory where I'd been working before, but it was clear that there was room for only one qualified chemist to stay on who was not serving in the armed forces. I was without work, but was rapidly called up to serve in the armed forces. My refusal to become a soldier of course meant that I was ordered to appear before a tribunal.

To my amazement the chairman introduced one of the two other members of the tribunal as a Quaker. "That means you can have no complaints. This hearing is being conducted in a spirit of total fairness." This was, however, a severe blow; I knew that there were some – not many, but some – Quakers who supported the war. The Quaker would have been selected for service on the tribunal precisely because he considered that however much Quakers were against war, they could not disobey the law of the land.

I made out my case to the best of my ability, saying that what I had to obey was not the law but my conscience, and that my conscience was based on a higher law.

The Quaker on the bench intervened. "Did not Jesus say 'I came not to send peace, but a sword'? Jesus calls us to the ultimate sacrifice, even as he himself was sacrificed."

I replied that the sword Jesus was referring to was not a physical sword but a spiritual sword, and that there were times when we would be called upon to stand apart for what we believed, just as I was attempting to do at that moment. I could not kill other human beings, and could in no circumstances see Jesus fighting in the trenches.

The chairman cut me short. "You have no idea what the trenches are like, you lily-livered coward, Evans. Those men in the trenches put you to shame. Don't you dare quote them in defence of your spinelessness."

" I do know what I am talking about. I have recently returned from the Front. I have served with the Friends Ambulance Unit. I have dragged hideously wounded men out of the mud. I have loaded them onto stretchers. I have watched them die before we could get them to an ambulance. I may not have been in the trenches themselves but shells often overshot their mark, creating huge craters, and we were in real danger. I have tended German soldiers as well as our own and found people every bit as decent and normal as ourselves. What we are doing to each other is lunacy. The courage I needed was not one of staying at the Front but of returning to stand up for what I believe in. That is why I am before this tribunal."

For a moment I thought the chairman looked at me with a new respect but it was no more than a brief calm before a veritable tornado.

He slammed his fist on the table. "What you need is to go back and see some real action!" he roared. I was refused any form of exemption from military service and was told to report to a military barracks.

On grounds of conscience I failed to present myself. I was arrested at home and taken to a police station, where I spent the night. The next day I appeared before a magistrate, was fined and then handed over to a military escort, which took me to the barracks to which I should have reported in the first place.

I was given a military uniform and told to put it on. I refused. I was punched and beaten, and two soldiers stuffed me barely conscious into the ill-fitting clothes. I was then flung into a dark cell, dripping with water and overrun with rats, for three days. Food consisted of one stale piece of bread every morning. There were three cells, one behind the other, dug into the hillside. The first cell received a pitiful amount of light through a small, filthy window. My cell and the third one beyond it had similar windows looking into the next cell and were both almost entirely dark. By the third day the prisoner in the third and darkest cell had gone mad.

I was dragged out of my cell and told to line up on the parade ground. Weak though I was, I refused. The sergeant went red in the face with fury and repeated the order. I'd only kept on my uniform because of the cold in the cell but now, instead of obeying the sergeant's order, began to take off my clothes in protest.

"Strip off your clothes, will you!" he shouted, ripping the shirt from my body. "Right, let's have you completely naked then!"

I was then kicked across the parade ground until I collapsed in a heap beside the soldiers being drilled. I realised that my knee was badly damaged and I haven't been able to walk properly to this day. There was more such treatment, which was so dreadful that some of the soldiers would even mutter as they went past us that they admired our spirit. One evening a soldier on guard duty even smuggled his own food into my cell.

We were threatened with being taken to France. This was in 1916. We would be taken in irons and placed on active service. If we continued to disobey we would be shot. There were seventeen of us. We were told to draw up our wills, but each and every one of us refused to do so. Under the extreme pressure, a few agreed to accept non-combatant duties. They were taken away and we did not see them again.

The rest of us were indeed taken to France. On arrival we were lined up on a huge parade ground. Orders were shouted for us to stand to attention, march and halt, but not one of us objectors moved. It was an extraordinary sight to see a thousand well-drilled soldiers obeying each command in such splendid unison, except for the straggly little groups of men left standing all over the parade ground.

I was taken to the Colonel's office. Partly because I was weak, and partly to make a point, I leant on his desk – something he was totally unaccustomed to. He shouted at me to stand to attention and grew angry when I would not address him as "Sir" or even "Mr", but simply called him by his name, "Henderson". He said that if I continued to refuse to fight I would be court-martialled and sentenced to death.

I replied that I did not recognise the right of the State to make me kill other people for my country, and so I also did not recognise any right that he might have to punish me, let alone hand down a sentence of death.

We were marched off under armed guard. One of the soldiers said in a low voice that it was a disgrace I could be threatened in this way. "I would never shoot you," he said. "I would rather shoot the officer who gave the order. I have come here to fight the Germans, not to kill Englishmen." I thanked him warmly, but said that my wish was to make peace with the Germans, not to kill them.

We were held in terrible conditions for several days at a camp near Boulogne. There were seventeen of us in one underground pit. Four of us were identified as the ringleaders. A captain came to tell me that he'd seen my papers and they'd been marked "death" in red at the top. "Do you really want to go through with this?" he asked me.

I replied: "Yes, I do. I have seen men dying in agony in the trenches for things that they believe in and I would not be less than them." The captain stepped back in surprise, looked me square in the eye and then came forward and shook me by the hand.

One morning we were taken out onto the parade ground to hear our sentences. "The charge is disobedience and failing to serve King and country." We were told that we were to "suffer death by being shot", then – after a pause – that this had been confirmed by the Commander-in-Chief but – another pause – that the sentence had been commuted to imprisonment for ten years.

We were returned to England. I did not, in fact, serve the ten-year sentence but appeared before more tribunals, went to various work-camps, was sentenced to hard labour and, once or twice, was held in more civilised conditions. I finished my last eight-month sentence just as the War came to an end.

All through this time, my resolve was tested to the utmost. I had to rely on spiritual forces to get me through, knowing that true freedom could only be defended by individuals prepared to act on what they believed, whatever the consequences. It wasn't exemption from military service that I sought, but to bear witness to the Truth as it was revealed to me. Peace began with each individual. It's odd that these were also some of the happiest times I have ever known!

When the war came to an end and I was released, I thought my troubles would be over. But now, it is as though people are more bitter than ever before. Apply for a job, and people want to know what you did during the War. Find out that you were a conscientious objector and they show you the door. I've been spat on in the street, shopkeepers have refused to serve me.

* * *

"So I am very grateful to you for listening and making me look normal again. Thank you too for the cup of tea," the young man concluded. "You will never know how much your kindness has meant to me. How much do I owe you?"

The barber had been cutting more and more slowly as he listened to the story. Now his fingers had ceased snipping and were resting gently on the young man's shoulders. They caught each other's eye in the mirror.

"It is I who am indebted to you, sir. There will be no charge."

# The Two Suns

Winter, in the East End of London. It was the late 1920s. The tall, stately young woman paused outside the school building. Some of the window panes were cracked and there was a general air of neglect. The school was squeezed in between a jam-making factory and a sack factory. It was foggy and damp, with the smell of coal and fish in the air. It was not exactly what she had imagined for her first teaching post.

Her mind went back to the day before. The director of the teacher training institute, Mr Endersby, had called her in to his office.

"You have done very well, Miss Burley," he said. "Indeed, it is precisely because you have done so well that we wonder whether you would be prepared to take on a rather awkward position we are having difficulty filling. It is at a primary school in Bethnal Green."

She knew that it would not be held against her if she refused the position, but the director read his would-be teacher correctly: she responded to a challenge and had a streak of Quaker idealism and stubbornness.

She thought for a moment and then replied, "I think I should like to go along and see the school tomorrow, and then I shall give you my reply."

She stood outside the school. It was out of term. The school was gaunt and silent. Her heart sank, and yet was stirred at the same time. As she stood there, a small boy came by on some errand. "Ain't no-one there, Miss," he said. "Got a few days 'oliday, we all 'ave."

"Is this your school?" she asked.

"No, Miss, it don' belong to me, but 'swhere I go," he replied cheekily.

"Well, perhaps one day you will own a big building like this," she smiled. "What's your name?"

"Tommy," he replied.

"Do you like your school, Tommy?" she said.

"Sawright," he said. "Like it when I can sit near the stove."

She looked at his raggedy shirt and saw that he wasn't wearing any shoes. "Why ever are you wearing bare feet in the middle of winter?" she exclaimed.

"Ain't got no shoes," came the answer. "Might get Tom's when he grows out of 'em."

"Well, let's hope that Tom grows very quickly," she said. "Now off you go, or you'll catch your death of cold."

"Sawright Miss, I'm used to it." And then, hesitating: "Are you the new teacher, Miss?"

Ruth knew that any sign of hesitation would be fatal. "Yes," she said as brightly as she could, "I'm the new face you'll be seeing in a few days time."

Coming as she did from a reasonably well-to-do background, Ruth was shocked by the poverty she found in the school, and in Bethnal Green. Nearly all the children came to school in bare feet, even on the coldest days. Their few clothes were patched. They were thin, pale and nearly all seemed to have coughs or colds they were unable to shake off.

One of the subjects that Ruth most looked forward to teaching was art. She soon realised that most of them had never done any drawing apart from scratching with chalky stones on the pavement. She thought back to all the art classes she had attended on her teacher training course. How astonished her teacher would have been to see this school, where none of the pupils had ever seen paints, let alone used them. She went to the headteacher but was told that there was no money for such luxuries.

One day, on her way back home from school, Ruth stopped at a shop selling art supplies. She had just received her first pay packet and asked to see a set of paints and brushes. The owner of the shop registered the flicker of dismay that crossed her face when she saw the price. "For a whole class, is it?" he said kindly. "In the East End, you say? Let me see now, I should be able to do a deal for a big order like that. In fact, Miss? – ah, Miss Burley – I've just been sent some new paints. I've been given a sample to try out. Why don't you take these along with the others and let me know how the children get on with them." Ruth walked out of the shop with her bag piled high with paints, brushes and crayons.

At the suggestion of the shopkeeper, she went to a wallpaper shop in Tottenham Court Road. She asked to speak to the manager. Mr Ford emerged from the back of the shop. She explained to him that she had just begun teaching at a school in the East End and was shocked to discover that there were no art materials. "And they are quite unable to afford such things themselves, as their parents don't even have the money for proper clothes and shoes.

"What I need is paper for them to draw and paint on. I understand that the cheapest possible paper is lining paper. If I were to buy some on a regular basis, could you give me a good price?"

Mr Ford momentarily turned away. Regaining his composure, he went to the back of the shop, returning with a large roll of paper. "This is spare," he said. "Please accept it with my compliments."

"Oh, but I couldn't," said Ruth. "I really must pay you. As it is, the owner of the art materials shop hardly allowed me to pay for anything."

But Mr Ford insisted. "Just bring me some of their paintings to see," he said.

The next day Ruth brought the art materials to the school. It was a grey, wet and miserable day. Raindrops ran down the cracked window panes. The children huddled their desks as close to the stove as they could, but even so most could not get warm.

In the afternoon she distributed the lining paper, cut neatly to size, together with the brushes and pots of paint: bright blues, reds, greens, yellows and blacks. "Now children, I want you all to paint whatever you like," she said. "But take your time and don't rush."

She looked at the children's eager faces as they dipped the brushes into the pots of paint with a sense of wonderment. The initial excitement and hubbub when she handed the materials out gave way to total silence apart from the sound of brushes moving across the paper.

Ruth went about the class. She came across a boy called Billy, whose page was still blank.

"Can't you think of anything to paint, Billy?" she said.

"Just thinking, Miss," he replied. "I'll be all right."

Ruth continued on around the room. Here and there she would make a suggestion or give a word of encouragement. When she came back to Billy, he was just getting started.

"And what have you decided to paint, Billy?" she asked.

"God."

"Oh, I see, God. But Billy, nobody knows what God looks like."

"They will when I've finished this," he replied.

Doing her best not to smile, Ruth moved on. That would be a story Mr Ford would enjoy next time she went to fetch lining paper from his shop. The rain continued to stream down the window panes. It was such a gloomy afternoon that it was almost impossible to see out.

She came to Tommy, who was just putting the finishing touches to his painting. "Why, that's lovely," said Ruth. "You've painted a beautiful tree with red apples and children in brightly coloured clothes running about and playing on the green grass. And here's a beautiful yellow sun on one side of the tree – and here's *another* beautiful yellow sun on the other side. That's very nice, but why Tommy have you painted *two* suns?"

Tommy looked up and stared out of the window for a moment. "I guess, Miss," he said, "it must be because it's such a lovely day."

# Facing the Tribunal

The long-bladed fan flickered lazily in the middle of the ceiling. The young man entered the Judge's chamber in the High Court in Accra. He was not invited to sit down, but had to stand in front of the large mahogany desk at which the Judge was seated. There was a man in a well-tailored tropical suit seated to the left of the Judge, and another to his right. They were not introduced, but Thurstan Shaw recognised one of them as a leading member of the business community in Ghana, or the Gold Coast as it was still known in 1939.

"You, Shaw," said the Judge, "have applied for registration as a conscientious objector. I trust you are aware of the gravity of this step. This is a time when every able-bodied man must be prepared to bear arms for King and country. The tribunal are disappointed that you should be taking this course of action."

"I am sorry that you should be disappointed, Sir. I can only act as my conscience tells me."

"What your conscience tells you and what it tells me and everyone else are two very different things. You have a position here at the University as a lecturer. As members of the expatriate community we have standards to uphold and an example to set. You are bringing dishonour on us all by refusing to be called up and perform military service. I am, however, required by law to ask you for your reasons. You will be aware that there are few grounds on which an exception can be made, and either you must be a member of a recognised religious group like the Quakers, or you would be exempted for being in essential work such as food production. I do not think that either applies in your case."

Thurstan Shaw had not been particularly nervous when he went to the High Court. He had a quiet inner confidence. He was doing the right thing and being true to himself. Nevertheless, he wished that the hearing could have been in public and that he might have had someone to assist him, as would have been the case had the hearing been held in England.

He was one of three people who were refusing to bear arms. There was a Quaker, a Methodist and himself. The Quaker, who was the first to go in, emerged from the meeting shaking with anger. It was not a quality Thurstan associated with the Quakers. His Quaker colleague could barely speak with rage about the insulting questions that had been put to him.

Thurstan knew that he was in for a tough hearing – but he was also forewarned. He resolved to do all he could to stay calm, and not to allow the tribunal to unsettle him.

"No," he replied, "I know the Quakers here and respect them, and they have been supportive of my stand, but I am not a Quaker." In his mind's eye he saw their highly characteristic meeting house, consisting as it did just of a thatched roof on four poles with no walls, in which he had sometimes held discussions with them. "As an anthropologist my interests do extend to studying the food production and diet of the Ibu people, but I doubt that you would regard that as a form of agricultural activity."

"Don't try to be clever, Shaw," said the Judge. "You face imprisonment if you refuse to be called up. On what grounds do you claim exemption?"

"I am asking for exemption purely on the grounds of my beliefs."

"Which are?"

"I have been brought up as a Christian. I am the son of a Church of England vicar, who taught me to be guided in life by love and fellow-feeling for other human beings. My model is Christ Jesus, whom I cannot see putting on a uniform and killing people."

There was a slight pause. The member of the panel to the left of the Judge murmured that however much Jesus's message might indeed have been one of love there were times when we had to confront evil, and this could mean bearing arms.

Grateful for the first sign of any understanding, Thurstan replied, "I know, Sir, that very difficult issues are involved. I do see both sides of the case and wrestle with my conscience as to how we should meet evil. But when Jesus talks about loving our enemies, I do not see how that is consistent with killing them."

The Judge pounced. "You say you are a member of the Church of England. You will, therefore, be aware that bishops of the church bless bombs and ships going into war. What do you say to that?"

"I can't help that!" exclaimed Thurstan. " All I can say is that I don't agree with them."

"What would you do if you saw a man attacking a child viciously? You would, I suppose, stand by idly?"

"There will always be rogues and knaves, and I believe in a good police force."

"I see, so you will let others do the dirty work for you. Is that where your cowardice takes you?"

Thurstan knew he was being baited. It was just such questions that had rattled his Quaker colleague. By keeping calm, he could make the members of the tribunal appear mean-spirited. He explained that he was not an out-and-out pacifist, but he could not contemplate himself killing people in cold blood. "As we human beings become more civilised, we must move away from the abomination of war. It is a primitive, deeply immoral way of settling differences."

"As someone who will not do their duty as required by the law, you are not in any position to lecture us about morality, Shaw," said the Judge.

Thurstan leaned forward towards the member of the tribunal who had shown some sympathy. "Sir, I think you understand my position and what I am trying to say. Someone must carry forward the banner showing that there is a better way. We cannot go on as we are. I grew up being told by my mother that the Great War would be the war to end all wars. But it lasted four years and millions died. Now, barely twenty years later, we are at war again. Two of my uncles suffered dreadfully in the trenches in the First World War. I saw the effects on their health and I am not prepared to inflict anything like that on people just because I, or they, are wearing a uniform."

"If it comes down to it, are you prepared to go to prison rather than fight?" asked the Judge.

"I cannot see that that would serve any purpose. But if that is the only way I can avoid acting against my conscience, then that is what I shall have to accept."

Thurstan did not lose his cool. The Judge continued to ask testing questions, but not quite so aggressively. Now and then the other members of the panel asked a question or made an observation. The hearing came to an end.

The Quaker's application for conscientious objector status was granted, but those of the Methodist and Thurstan were refused. Not long afterwards, the Methodist was called up and joined the army. Thurstan spent the rest of the War in Accra waiting to be called up, but no papers were ever served on him. He did not find out why.

Years later, after he had become a Quaker, Thurstan happened to come across a man who was an official in the Colonial Secretary's office in Accra when the war broke out. He recalled Thurstan's case. When Thurstan asked if he remembered why he had not been called up, the official replied, "Whatever their own views, and however much they may have disagreed with you, I rather think the tribunal may have been impressed by what you said."

# The Choice

The old man on the beach was lost in thought. Through his half-closed eyes he could just make out the light dancing on the waves and the children playing in the sand, but he didn't really take them in. It was all so long ago, and yet he recalled the events with total clarity. Indeed, the memories had never left him in all those fifty years.

Anton de Wit was a young man at the time, working as a teacher in a primary school in the Oosterpark neighbourhood of Amsterdam. It was his first teaching position. The school was just a few minutes walk from the River Amstel. It was located in a Jewish area, and many of children in his class were Jewish: Shamay, Miriam, Rebecca, David, Joseph, Nora. He had learned quite a bit about their customs and become friendly with many of the families. In turn, he would share with them some of the things he loved about Quakerism, for his mother had been an English Quaker who married a Dutch pharmacist. He would tell his Jewish friends about the silent meetings and about the importance they attached to living peacefully, truthfully and simply.

It was a lively area. On Sundays there was a famous market. People would come from all over Holland to watch people like Professor Kokadorus, who could sell anything to anyone. He would slice leeks up very finely and wrap them in cigarette paper. These he would sell as pills against toothache. Anyone suffering from toothache was invited to come forward and chew on a pill, rinse their mouth with a glass of water and spit everything out into a bowl. Professor Kokadorus would then point triumphantly to the "little white worms" floating in the water, which he said were worms that came from bad teeth. He sold lots of pills.

It was 1942. Holland was occupied by Germany. Life had become increasingly difficult for Jews: they had to wear big yellow stars in public and were even not allowed to ride bicycles. Reports reached them of Jews being rounded up in Paris and sent to mysterious "labour camps". Later, in the summer, Dutch Jews began to be seized and deported by train.

One morning, Anton came to school to find that Miriam and Joseph had gone. Anton knew better than to ask questions but later heard that they were in hiding with a non-Jewish family in the neighbourhood. He knew of several other Dutch families who had taken in Jewish children. Meanwhile, more and more children were being taken away with their families. His class had a lot of empty desks.

The non-Jewish Dutch people too lived in fear. There were stories of people being shot for refusing to co-operate with the German authorities.

Early one evening in September, German soldiers burst into the house where Anton lived in the Camperstraat and came to his flat on the second floor.

"You are Anton de Wit, the schoolteacher, are you not?" one of the young soldiers demanded.

"I am," replied Anton as calmly as he could, although inwardly he was shaking.

"We know that Jewish children are being hidden in this neighbourhood," went on the soldier. "Where they are being held?"

A thousand thoughts went through Anton's mind at once. He could deny all knowledge, but that would go against the testimony to truth. He could tell what he knew, and almost certainly send the children and those hiding them to their death. Or he could try avoiding the question.

"People here are very careful not to say anything that other people do not need to know," he replied.

"As schoolteacher you will know where they are. Give us their names and addresses and no harm will come to you," said the soldier with an edge of menace.

"There are so many rumours," said Anton. "We hear stories that some people have fled to England by boat in the dead of night."

"We are not interested in rumours but in what you know," said the soldier, grasping him by his jacket and shaking him violently. The next moment a rifle butt came crashing down on his head and he found himself being dragged down the stairs and along the street, where he was taken to a special unit for questioning.

They held him for three days. He was shouted at, pummelled and beaten repeatedly. They asked him about the Dutch resistance movement and questioned him about Quakerism. During the brief moments when they left him alone he was tormented by the question of telling the truth. His mother and the Quakers always stressed that the best course of action was simply to tell the truth. But this was not a truth that the soldiers needed to know. It was a truth they would use for bad purposes. Was there a greater Truth to which he should be true? Were there, in fact, no rules and would he have to decide for himself what was right?

It would have been so much easier to give in. He knew of people who had. Whole families were taken away as a result. No-one, at that time, knew exactly what would happen to the people taken away, but they had a reasonably good idea. But Quakerism meant so much to him. Everything he truly valued could be found in the shared silence. And there, at the centre, were peace and simplicity and equality – and truth.

But was truth the same as truthfulness? And did you still have to be truthful in such extraordinary circumstances? Then again, by telling the truth he would be sticking to his principles and could be sure of saving his own life, while not really knowing what would happen to those whose names he mentioned. What the soldiers did with the information was not his responsibility.

Just as he was trying to order his thoughts, the door to his cell would swing open again and he would be hauled out to sit on a small wooden bench under a fierce light. Once again the direct question came: "Do you know where Jewish children are being held, yes or no?"

If he replied "no" they would know he was lying. They were right: as schoolteacher in the closely-knit community he would know what was going on, even though he was not a Jew.

Once again he tried evading the question. "One hears so many vague things."

The German officer questioning him erupted in fury. "We are not interested in vague things! You say you are a Quaker and that you believe in truth. Yes or no, do you know where the children are being held?" he shouted.

This was the moment of truth. He longed to say yes, to tell what he knew and just to go home. It would be so easy. People would understand. If not he could leave the neighbourhood. Tell the truth? Lie? Evade? What should he do?

Once again the rifle butt came down on his head. Everything went black. When he regained consciousness he was lying on the floor. The room was empty. He heard voices in the corridor: "Van Velzen has cracked. We have the information we need. Private Becker, get rid of that idiot Quaker."

His head caked in blood, Anton found himself escorted back to his flat by a German soldier. The young man propped him up as they walked slowly, stopping to sit on a bench under a tree. "I have never met a Quaker before," said the soldier in surprisingly good Dutch. "I was touched by what you said about peacefulness and that of God in every one. I hate this war."

\* \* \*

In all the years that followed Anton de Wit replayed the events over and over in his mind. As it happened, someone else had given the German soldiers the information they wanted. Jewish children were found and taken away, although Anton was sure that there were also some, like Nora, who hadn't been found. Looking back, he now wondered whether the right thing would have been to lie and say there were no children in hiding. That would have meant facing torture and possibly death. But that would not have been true to his principles of telling the truth.

So perhaps he had been right to try not telling the truth without lying either. What he was clear about was that to have told the truth in these circumstances would have been wrong. There was a higher truth he had to obey. There were no definite rules.

He also often wondered whether, like some of his friends, he should have joined the Dutch resistance to fight the occupation. Had it been cowardly not to do so? He had certainly helped the resistance, for example arranging for two of the children to escape to England by boat. But he had never felt able to join the resistance properly as this would have meant turning his back on non-violence.

Still tormented by all these thoughts, Anton decided, fifty years after the events, to return to the neighbourhood in Amsterdam where he had once taught. After the War he had never felt able to go back there again.

After making inquiries in local shops and at the school, he found to his surprise that the head of the Oosterpark resistance was not only alive but still living in the area.

And so it was that, half a century on, the two men sat outside one sunny summer afternoon on a bench discussing those distant events. After they had spoken at length, Anton said, "You know, this is the very bench on which I collapsed when being escorted home by a German soldier. I even remember his name – it was Becker."

Piet Hartog started. "Becker?" he said. "A German soldier who spoke good Dutch?"

"Yes, he did," replied Anton. "Did you come across him?"

"I did. Let me tell you the story. He saved my daughter's life."

\* \* \*

You will recall that I ran a bakery. One day, a year or so after the war had ended, a man came into the shop right at the end of the day just as I was to lock up. He looked nervous. I recognised him straight away.

"My name is Becker – Heinrich Becker," he said slowly in heavily accented but good Dutch. "You must say if I am not welcome, for I was stationed here in this part of Amsterdam with the occupying forces. I felt I had to return and say how sorry I was for everything that happened."

"My name is Hartog," I replied, "Piet Hartog. I always said that I would never let another German person into my house as long as I lived, but you are the one exception. You saved my daughter Evelien's life. We wanted to speak to you about it afterwards, but it was too dangerous and in any case you were moved away not long after that. Why – what made you do it?"

"It is hard for me to explain why I have come. I am not quite sure that I know myself. I think I had to return to the place where it happened.

"Where to start? Perhaps you need to know a little about me. I come from the Rhineland. I grew up in a small village near Bonn. We had an apple orchard and my father and mother ran the local tavern. Like all my school friends I went into the army when war broke out. I was just 18. I was sent to Amsterdam not long after Germany invaded Holland in 1941. I spent over two years there: an unusually long time, because Holland fascinated me and I decided to learn the language. Our languages have much in common, so it was not difficult but, even so, I was one of the very few to make the effort. That meant I could read Dutch documents and, after a while, I was even able to interview people in their own language. It gave me a glimpse into the Dutch way of life which few other soldiers had. I also became valuable to the army as one of its few fluent Dutch speakers.

"We did not know it at the time, but the war was nearly over. We did, however, know that things were starting to go against us, and the Dutch Resistance was getting ever bolder. Orders came through to make more frequent and stricter searches.

"On the day we are talking about, I was assigned to a roadblock we had set up just a few streets away from here in the Camperstraat. I had only just come on duty early in the morning. A girl came round the corner on a bicycle. She was in a nurse's uniform, and I recognised her as the girl from the bakery, who often made deliveries of bread early in the morning. This morning, too, her basket was full of loaves and rolls.

"We had often waved her through before but with our orders to be stricter I signalled to her to stop. My colleagues were busy searching a van. Other bicycles were not stopped as we did not have enough people, so I suppose you could say that your daughter was unlucky.

"You will recall that it was a cold morning, in late winter. Puddles had turned to ice. When she stopped she smiled at me and said, 'I'm late. I just have to make these deliveries and then get to the hospital.'

"Something didn't feel quite right to me. I began lifting up the loaves and rolls. Your daughter – Evelien – became very talkative, saying how cold it must be for me to be on duty and how was it that I spoke Dutch, but I just kept going through the bike basket. When I got to the bottom I could tell that she was becoming very nervous. I saw two cylindrical objects wrapped in tea towels. 'Oh, they're some special rolls,' she said. 'I'm trying to keep them warm.' But when I felt them they were cold and hard and as I unfolded the tea towel to reveal a corner of the contents I knew straight away what they were: pistols.

"My first reaction was to call out to my colleagues and summon the lieutenant. The pale, pink morning sunlight was lighting up the bricks of the houses and playing on the frozen puddles. Time, somehow, became frozen too. You know how they say that if you are suddenly faced by death all sorts of thoughts flash through your mind and you can see your whole life go by – well, it was a bit like that. One part of me was thinking about calling the lieutenant and mentally I could already see this young woman being put up against the wall on which the sunlight was playing and being shot. Then we would march straight round to the bakery and round up everyone there, interrogate them and shoot another ten or twelve people by way of example. I could picture an entire family being wiped out. As it was, many Jewish people from pre-cisely that part of Amsterdam had been taken away a year or so earlier. I saw that community ripped apart. Whole houses were left empty.

"Most of all, though, I was conscious of the young woman facing me. She, like me, was in a uniform – in her case, a nurse's uniform. She was doing a job, just as I was doing a job. In that tiny split second, I wondered about her life and could not help but admire her courage at running such a risk.

"I realised too that, at that moment, I had a choice. The young woman's life was in my hands. Here was someone whose life was still before her and who displayed courage and devotion to a cause. And yet – what she was doing would cause violence too. I had seen enough violence, and remembered how the schoolteacher we had questioned spoke about believing that peace started with each of us, in our hearts.

"I folded the tea towel back into place. 'Mustn't let them get cold,' I heard myself saying. 'You be on your way now, and take care, it's slippery!'

"Your daughter gave me a look I shall never forget. It combined astonishment, fear, relief, wonder and an extraordinary sense of connection, as though she knew what was going through my mind. It was a kind of pity, but not quite that; more that we were both caught up in something and being forced to do certain things, and a recognition that just as she had chosen to take a risk so now I too had chosen an unexpected course of action.

"I still cannot quite explain why I acted as I did. All I know is that what I did has stayed with me powerfully ever since. I cannot tell you what a relief it was for me when the war came to an end. And now I have come back here, because it was in these backstreets that I discovered hope."

\* \* \*

The old man opened his eyes. It was growing dark and the beach was largely deserted. Here and there the incoming tide was lapping at the sandcastles the children had made. He almost expected to find himself still sitting on the bench with Piet Hartog, as he had been the day before.

"Yes," he said to himself, "he was the true Quaker, soldier or not. It was he who lived out his truth. And perhaps that is what matters most."

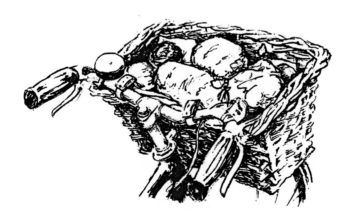

# The Extra Mile

Steve and Hank lashed down the last of the timber that had been heaved onto the truck. It was late afternoon. Their Italian helpers from the village cheered and passed round a bottle of water. There was no tea, and no coffee, for it was 1946, just a year after the Second World War had come to an end, and such luxuries were still in pitifully short supply in Italy. The two men, both American Quakers, sat down for a moment on some rubble to get their breath back. Hank had been there for some time and spoke a little Italian but Steve, who was visiting relief teams all over Europe on behalf of the American Friends Service Committee in Philadelphia, did not.

"What's he saying?" Steve asked Hank after a local man, arms pumping wildly, had made what appeared to be a short speech.

"Not quite sure," replied Hank, "but I think Luigi's thanking us for taking the timber up the mountain and warning us to watch out as the villagers there aren't to be trusted."

There was a lot of backslapping and some further cheering as the two young men climbed into the cab of the truck. At the third try the engine spluttered into life. With Hank at the wheel the truck lurched out of the village.

"Conditions here are even worse than I was expecting," observed Steve as they drove off. "I'd been told there were a lot of people who had fled from their homes during the war and who were returning now, but I'd no idea so many houses were flattened. And just look at these roads."

Hank picked his way carefully along the potholed road. Some of the craters were deep enough for a truck to get stuck or break an axle. Slowly, the road improved as they drew clear of the village and reached the countryside where the shelling had been less intense.

"A lot of them have nowhere to live, hardly anything to eat, and just the clothes on their backs," said Hank. "And yet look at the way they are rebuilding their houses with almost no tools. Everything has to be done by hand but I've never seen people work harder."

"It's a real shame that they are still so distrustful of the people in Colledemacini," said Steve. "You'd think they'd all want to work together in their hour of need."

"Those two villages, one in the hills and one on the plains, have been feuding for hundreds of years. And now in this war they found themselves on different sides. On top of that, everyone here was lied to by the government and deceived for years. So it's been a great thing to get them to agree to this truckload of timber at all."

Steve's thoughts went back to the previous evening, when he had first arrived in the Aventino Valley. He and Hank had sat around a rough wooden table in a makeshift cafe with five of the local men. Luigi, who had a smattering of English, was their leader. Steve put him at around 35, and he was obviously a forceful and determined man.

He had certainly been the hardest to persuade. The situation was obvious: the village of Colledemacini, which had also been wrecked by the war, needed timber from the plains, while it could supply the limestone that was so badly needed in the plains to make cement in the kilns. Now, with refugees streaming back and so much poverty and so much rebuilding to be done, was it not possible that they could put aside old hatreds and work together?

But the trust simply wasn't there and the communities hadn't found a way to co-operate. Hank had been going backwards and forwards between the two villages. He told the gathering of men that Colledemacini was prepared to exchange a load of limestone for a load of timber.

Most of the men seemed cautiously in favour of going ahead with the deal. Steve didn't need to speak Italian to know what they were saying. Two of them, Mario and Giovanni, pointed to the gaping hole in one wall of the cafe and to the rubble outside in the streets and the rebuilding that was taking place. They had stone, but no cement. It was spring; it was time to crack on with the building work.

Luigi grew very excited. He slammed the table with his fist. "They big liars!" he shouted. "We send wood but truck he come back empty, wait and see. You ask chicken to put neck in fox mouth." He tapped his head rapidly with two fingers: "Stupido."

The word fox made Steve think of George Fox and how he spoke of "walking cheerfully over the world, answering that of God in everyone."

Somehow, he did not think that this would impress Luigi.

Maybe, he thought as they jolted along in the truck, the turning point had been when he had remembered the cigarettes he had brought with him. People used cigarettes instead of money on the black market at the time, but Steve refused to do so. Instead, he opened a packet and handed them around. There was a silence as everyone lit up. Hank caught Steve trying not to laugh. "What's the joke?" he said. "The silence," replied Steve. "Reminds me of a Quaker meeting."

Luigi had caught the word silence and they had to explain. For a while they all forgot about mistrust and timber and limestone and broken down trucks, about bad roads and lack of petrol, and instead spoke of sitting in silence for a whole hour except when someone felt moved to speak. "I know it sounds crazy to be talking about meeting in silence," said Steve. "You've just been through years of war, most of you have lost your houses, and your country has been torn apart. And yet it's not just something for when times are good and easy. A lot of our guys were imprisoned right at the beginning three hundred years ago, and we were widely hated and mistrusted."

The others were genuinely interested and asked many questions. Slowly, they returned to the matter at hand. "Look," said Luigi. "If you thinking you can fix this – perhaps I trust you. Maybe you no succeed, but you try, we believe you."

Steve's attention returned to the truck which was still bouncing up and down, even though the road had improved. They were driving along the Aventino Valley. "You must have done pretty well to persuade those guys up in the hills," he mused.

"Wasn't easy," Hank conceded, "but if anything it's even worse up there, they're so remote and cut off. Got enough cigarettes for them as well? Might need them in case they change their minds."

It was at that point that the truck went over a hole, which Hank saw too late. There was a bang, the truck lurched and Hank brought the vehicle to a stop.

"Oh my sainted forefathers. That's one granddaddy of a blow-out. We ain't going no further tonight."

"What about the spare?" asked Steve.

"Spare? There is no spare. It's hard enough just getting hold of tyres."

"Well, there's nothing for it but to walk back to the village. We'll have to get it fixed in the morning and go up to Colledemacini just as soon as we can, perhaps tomorrow."

"No way," replied Hank. "You saw it last night with your own eyes – these people have had a belly-full of being lied to. The people up in the hills in Colledemacini are just as distrustful as this lot. I gave them an undertaking that we would be bringing them the timber today, even if it got late. All I've got going for me around here is my word. I either keep it or explain why I can't. Otherwise, I might just as well pack up and go back to Baltimore. We'll just have to walk."

"How far is it?"

"About fifteen miles, I'd reckon."

"We better get going."

The two men set off. All they had between them was two apples. Neither complained about feeling hungry and Steve not once asked how much further they had to go. The road was rough and full of winding bends that turned back on themselves. Every now and then, as the stony road grew steeper, they would stop and rest for a minute. Here and there they had magnificent views back down the valley in the moonlight. From time to time they came across a small stream by the side of the road where they could cup their hands and have a drink.

"We should each have carried a log, Steve. Would've made a good impression."

"Yeh, we don't even have backpacks. Can't imagine why we didn't think of that. And it's such a gentle climb."

The bends seemed unending. Hour after hour they continued to climb. At last they were able to see that the vegetation was thinning slightly.

It was approaching midnight when they rounded yet another bend: suddenly, a ghostly church spire loomed up. Reaching heavenward and surrounded by ruins in the milky light, the steeple served as a strange symbol of hope. There was not a soul to be seen, although here and there lights flickered in cellars, where the families who had returned were now living.

They picked their way through the piles of rubble in the street – this village, too, had been shelled – and made their way to the village square and a house that was still reasonably intact.

"I think this is where the mayor lives," explained Hank. He knocked on the door. After a short pause a window flew open upstairs and a head looked out. "Chi è?" came a voice.

"Hank, and a friend."

"Hank? Americano Hank?" The window slammed to and there was the sound of feet coming swiftly down the stairs. The heavy door swung open, to reveal the mayor, lantern in hand.

"We were expecting you hours ago!" said the mayor.

"I'm sorry," said Hank, "but our truck broke down in the foothills. I knew you would be worried, which is why my friend Steve and I have come to tell you."

"On foot?"

"Yes, there was no other way."

"Do you mean to say," said the mayor slowly, "that you have walked all this way just to tell me that you weren't able to come with the truck?"

The mayor whispered something to his ten-year-old son, who by now had also appeared at the door. Moments later the bell in the church began ringing. Soon the entire village had turned out in the square before the mayor's house.

"These people from America," said the mayor in a loud voice, "Hank and Steve, have been walking for the last five or six hours to tell us that the load of timber we were expecting is on its way but the truck has broken down. They did not want us to think that we had been let down. My friends – this is something to celebrate."

The mayor disappeared into his cellar, reappearing shortly with some large flasks of wine. Others produced sausage and coarse bread. Someone struck up an accordion and people began singing, dancing and laughing. Speeches were made and toasts drunk until, with dawn not far away, they said goodbye. It was time to go back down the mountain. The mayor and a few others led Steve and Hank down a direct path avoiding all the bends in the road.

In the last of the moonlight, they embraced and took leave of one another where the path met the straight road at the foot of the mountain. "We'll have that wheel fixed and get the load of timber to you later today," said Steve.

"You boys get some sleep first," said the mayor. "The timber can wait. Those bends are tricky, remember! You are more important to us than a few logs. Come tomorrow – and bring Luigi and some of his friends. We'll have another party."

# The Roll-Call

The new girl was eight. She came from France. She had arrived in Ireland with a very small suitcase and was nervous and shy.

The day before she came, John Brigham, the young headmaster of the Quaker boarding school in Waterford, spoke to the school after roll-call. "Now dear children, we have a new girl coming tomorrow. She is called Anna, and is French. Anna is a Hebrew name. It means grace, charm and mercy." He paused. "Anna was found alive in one of the concentration camps at the end of the war a few months ago. She was the only member of her family to survive. She has been staying with a Quaker family in England. If she seems a little different from the rest of you, you will know why. I am sure you will be kind and thoughtful."

To begin with Anna was thin, sad and withdrawn. The other children, however, did all they could to include her in everything they did, while doing their best not to make her feel different. They took her through the woods to the spot where it was possible to cross the little river by jumping from stone to stone. They took her up a hill from where they could see Waterford Bay in the distance. She joined in running races and loved craftwork. Her English improved in leaps and bounds. Instead of being shy, she became one of the liveliest girls in the school, always dashing about excitedly and having fun. There seemed no end to her energy.

To begin with, the other children would sometimes ask her where she had been before she came to the Newtown School. She would tell them that she was from a mountainous part in the south of France, but then she would stop. Much though they wanted to know, the children soon learned never to ask her anything about the war or the concentration camps. If ever they did a blank look would settle over Anna's face and in moments she would start doing something energetic, such as leading them in an elaborate game of hide-and-seek or tag.

The children stopped asking and Anna was quickly accepted and seemed just like any other girl in the school.

Except for one thing. Every morning, there was roll-call. The whole school, boarders and day pupils alike, were required to turn out in the quadrangle first thing before school. Their names would be called out one by one by the head boy. Sometimes, if it was very wet, the roll-call would be held in the gymnasium.

Each time, Anna would be unable to answer when her name was called. She was clearly upset, although she tried to conceal it. She would soon appear to be herself again, but John Brigham realised that the roll-call would be taking her back to the freezing parade ground in the concentration camp, where the prisoners had to line up each morning as their numbers were called out by the guards.

When John tried to talk to Anna about it her face would go blank. He told Anna that it would be all right if she didn't join in the roll-call, but she shook her head and continued coming.

But still Anna was unable to reply when the head boy called out her name. It began to set her apart from the others. John consulted the other teachers, made the roll-call as short as possible and tried once again to talk with Anna. His wife Pat spoke to her. Nothing helped.

At last he approached the head boy. John trusted the head boy; it was a school with few rules, in which each individual was valued and everyone took responsibility for maintaining the high standards of behaviour. There was no gulf between the teachers and the pupils but a sense that everyone worked together, in their different ways.

"I don't know what to do about Anna," he said. "The roll-call continues to affect her badly. Perhaps we should stop having a roll-call altogether, but that would only draw even more attention to her."

"Leave it with me," said the head boy, after they had spoken for a while.

The next morning, it was Anna who was standing in front of the rows of children. At first hesitantly, and then more strongly, she called the roll.

# The Dress Suit

There was a lack of energy in the room. No-one was talking. People were slumped in chairs and trying to read, but in fact they were each lost in their own thoughts. They had all started out with such good intentions, and there was so much to do. There were so many refugees, orphans, displaced soldiers and former prisoners of war. Many people needed clothing and were homeless. Whole cities had been flattened. There was widespread hunger. Europe was in ruins.

In the past, Quakers had managed to do so much. After the First World War, they had helped distribute food to sick and hungry children in Germany. They had helped heal broken communities and had brought education in Russia and Poland.

But now, it was all going wrong. There were shortages of essential materials. Supplies were not getting through. Trucks had flat tyres that could not be fixed. Communication was almost impossible. When they learned what had happened to the Jews in the concentration camps, people in France and Poland were in no mood to forgive or reach out.

Those in charge of the Quaker relief effort in the various parts of Europe were called to Amsterdam for a conference to discuss the difficulties they all faced. The more they heard from each other, the more discouraged they became.

It was the last afternoon of the four-day conference. The Friends, mainly young and mainly American and British but also drawn from many other countries, faced the prospect of returning to their scattered and isolated teams. Far from giving them fresh determination and hope, the conference made it all the more clear that the task was beyond them: there was too much misery and chaos, too little money and goodwill, and too few workers.

As they were sitting around dejectedly, the door burst open. It was a Dutch Friend, holding a newspaper. "We've been given the Nobel Peace

Prize!" he all but shouted. "Look at this headline: *Quakers honoured for relief service.*"

Everyone sat there silently in stunned amazement. Later, they would all say how they had been on the point of leaping to their feet and cheering and hugging one another when the silence took over. They fell into a Meeting for Worship. Only one person spoke, a young woman working in Poland: "All I can say is – a little love goes a long way."

\* \* \*

The Nobel Committee awarded the prize to two organizations, as representing Quakers: the Friends Service Council in London, and the American Friends Service Committee in Philadelphia. Being their chairman, Henry Cadbury was going to represent the Americans at the prizegiving ceremony in Oslo on the 10th of December 1947. He went to see the secretary of the Committee, Clarence Pickett.

"Clarence, this is all very well, but have you seen what I am expected to wear? It's full evening dress, with tails. I have no such suit and indeed have never worn tails in my life!"

"Well, Friend, I'm sure that we can find you some."

"No, that would not be right. Can you imagine George Fox in tails?" he chuckled. "No, simplicity means that I go as I am, in no more than an ordinary suit."

"But that would be to embarrass our hosts. Don't forget that they have only given us the prize because they have looked carefully into who we are and what we stand for. Why don't we ask the Clothing Department whether they have something?"

"The Clothing Department?" said Henry in astonishment. "But they collect clothes for refugees."

"We're given the oddest things by members of the public. It's worth a try," said Clarence, picking up the phone. "Clothing Department? Yes, Clarence Pickett here. I know this is a strange inquiry, but I am wondering whether by any chance you have a dress suit, with tails. Yes! I'll hold while you look."

He held his hand over the phone. "She's gone off to have a look. She thinks they might."

And so it was that Henry Cadbury found himself fitted out in a dress suit that happened to fit perfectly.

At the ceremony, Henry Cadbury heard the chairman of the Nobel Committee say in his speech that he thought Quakers deserved the peace prize because "It is through the silent help from the nameless to the nameless that they have worked to promote brotherhood among nations.

"Back in 1660 Quakers said, 'We utterly deny all outward wars and strife and fightings with outward weapons, for any end and under any pretence whatsoever. And this is our testimony to the whole world.' But that goes much further than a refusal to take part in war. It leads to this: it is better to suffer injustice than to commit injustice. It is from within people themselves that victory must in the end be gained. You have shown the world that it is possible to build up in a spirit of love what has been destroyed in a spirit of hatred.

"It is in the spirit in which this work is performed that Quakers have given the most to the people they have met. 'We weren't sent out to make converts', a young Quaker has said: 'we've come out for a definite purpose, to build up in a spirit of love what has been destroyed in a spirit of hatred. We're not missionaries. We can't tell if even one person will be converted to Quakerism. We have not come out to show the world how wonderful we are. No, the thing that seems most important is the fact that while the world is waging a war in the name of Christ, we can bind up the wounds of war in the name of Christ. Religion means very little until it is translated into positive action.'"

The chairman ended by quoting some lines from a Norwegian poem:

> The unarmed only
> Can draw on sources eternal.
> The spirit alone gives victory.

In reply, Henry Cadbury said, "Many people say to us: 'It is not the food or the clothing that really affects us most. It is the confidence in other people, the belief that somebody cares, that affects us most.' We believe that war is a moral problem and that the force of religion is essential to its solution."

At the reception afterwards, Henry felt ill at ease in his tails. A constant stream of people came up to him and his British counterpart, Margaret Backhouse, to offer their congratulations. At last it seemed that all the handshaking had been done. Just as he was helping himself to an orange juice, a distinguished-looking man took him to one side. It turned out to be a former German ambassador who had fled to Sweden.

"You look very fine in that costume," he remarked, "but I expect it is not something that Quakers wear very often?"

"Indeed not," replied Henry. "I have never worn such a suit of clothes in my entire life, and can't say that I feel comfortable in it."

"At least you don't have to wear a hat!" joked the ambassador. "Didn't Quakers once make a point of not taking their hats off to show that everyone was equal?"

"You are very well-informed, friend," replied Henry. "I thought that very few people outside of Britain had ever heard of Quakers. I was impressed how much the chairman of the Nobel Peace Prize committee had found out about Quakerism."

"In my case it was easier, for I had first-hand experience of Quakers in Germany. This was just after the First World War. It is hard to describe just how bad conditions were then. I well remember what we called *Quäkerspeisung* – the food parcels that saved our lives. Now you are organising the same relief action again, and another generation of Germans will always remember you."

The ambassador shifted his weight awkwardly from one foot to another. "I really came over not just to thank you, but to express my deep regrets. It has only been because of the actions of my country that your wonderful work has been needed in the first place."

"I greatly appreciate what you say," said Henry, "but we all share responsibility. Victory in war can make real peace difficult. Victory is not the same thing as peace; it is then that true peace must be built. It is not merely a matter of mopping up the world after war."

"No," said the ambassador, "it is now that we are sowing the seeds of a future war or a future peace."

"It is strange – far from thinking that we were succeeding, many of our Quaker peace workers had become most discouraged by all the difficulties they were facing here in Europe: the lack of transport and basic supplies, and all the hatred and suspicion. It came to us as a great surprise to be awarded this."

"To me, what you are showing is that peace can only start with each one of us, as individuals," observed the ambassador. "But it is very difficult to bring that about when there is still so much anger and mistrust."

"Another great difficulty is getting governments to do what they don't want to do. But we find that with governments too, what cannot be done publicly can often be done privately face to face, sometimes where you least expect to find help. You expressed your regret for what your country did, but during the War we had some extraordinary experiences with Nazi officials, who sometimes went to great lengths to help us behind the scenes. When it comes to individual people, they often understand what you are about, and can be prepared to take real risks in the name of humanity."

"Perhaps," observed the ambassador, "some of those very officials had their lives saved in Germany in the early 1920s by the same efforts from which I benefited. You Quakers built up quite a reputation at that time. Your example was on my mind when I fled the country."

They were joined by Margaret Backhouse. "It's sometimes said that Quakers can do anything, but we're ordinary people just longing for peace like everyone else," she said. "Often it's a matter of acting as a bridge and bringing the human spirit and higher forces together.

"Let me give you an example. The French government invited a Quaker delegation to France not long before the end of the war. A well-known writer told them about fifty tons of clothing that were available for Polish refugees. But the Quakers in the team explained that their job this time was with the French. They noted the information politely, but regretted that they couldn't help.

"A few weeks later, they reached Paris. Here, they were hauled before the American and British military authorities and asked to explain what they were doing. The war was still continuing, and the Allied forces were worried about any civilians who might get in the way of the final war effort.

"To begin with, the colonel who interviewed them was stern and cold. But the more they spoke, the more he realised they were taking real risks and doing what they could to bring people together once the war came to an end, and provide them with practical help. So the colonel began to relax.

" 'You know,' he said, 'we're going to need a great deal of relief work once this war is over, which it soon will be. Right now a problem that is really worrying me is the presence of fifty thousand Polish refugees in the Ardennes north of here. These people have nothing, no food, no housing, no clothing.'

" 'We know where there are fifty tons of clothing meant for displaced Polish people,' exclaimed one of the delegation. And so the problem was solved, and Quakers got the credit. The clothes were distributed, and of course once again it seemed that Quakers could do anything!"

\* \* \*

Whether there were any dress suits with tails among those fifty tons we shall never know. Nor shall we shall ever find out what happened to the dress suit Henry Cadbury wore in Oslo, but it will have been put to good use: on return to Philadelphia it was sent off in the next Friends Service Committee consignment of clothes for refugees in Europe. However strange it may have looked, it will have brought warmth and protection and perhaps even a smile to the face of the wearer, digging potatoes in some far-flung field in war-ravaged Europe.

# A Brush with the Law

"Maude, you can't possibly stop to pick up that man."

"Why ever not? It's a hot day and he looks as though he's been standing there for ages," said Maude, bringing the car to a standstill and waiting for a gap in the traffic so that she could turn round. "The French never give anybody a lift."

"But – well, I just don't like the look of him, that's all."

"He's French, Dorothy. Besides, you're a Quaker prison minister and mix with all sorts. You'll just have to see that of God in him."

With a disregard for the traffic of which a Frenchman would have been proud, Maude performed a U-turn, drove back a hundred yards and pulled up opposite where the man was still standing. Leaning across her companion, she motioned with her hand, pointing first at the man and then at the empty backseat of the Morris Minor.

The Frenchman's face lit up and he nodded in understanding. Maude executed another expert manoeuvre and brought the car to a halt at the precise point where the man had been standing, while simultaneously the Frenchman was nipping across the road. They found themselves on opposite sides again.

He looked at the car with astonishment. Then, nimbly dodging a huge Frenchman perched precariously but unconcernedly on a tiny scooter, he doubled back across the road and appeared at Maude's window – which, as her car was a British one, was on the pavement side.

"Where do you want to go to?" she asked in French before the man had a chance to open his mouth.

"Wherever you are going, madame?" he said.

"It's not where we're going but where you want to go," said Maude. "We're going to Lille."

"Ah, Lille, yes, that would suit me very fine," he said, opening the door and getting in.

"You must know where you're going," said Maude firmly as the man settled into the back seat with his small kitbag.

"To a ship that is not bound for any port, all winds are the right wind, madame."

"Monsieur, you are a philosopher," she replied. But Dorothy, half-looking over her shoulder, whispered to Maude, "He may be a philosopher, but if you ask me he is also a jailbird."

The Frenchman was apparently possessed of extraordinarily sharp hearing, and also spoke some English.

"Bird? Jailbird? *Qu'est-ce que c'est*, un jailbird?"

Maude shot Dorothy a get-out-of-that-one look.

Dorothy reflected for a moment on the Testimony to Truth and then, taking a deep breath, said, "A jailbird, monsieur, is another name for a prisoner."

"You think I am a *prisonnier*, madame – and, madame, you are right. *Mais* – how can you tell?"

"Well, in the first place, you're hitchhiking, so you probably don't have much money. And then, you see, I'm a prison chaplain, and come across a lot of prisoners and I couldn't help noticing that your hand and forearm are heavily tattooed. Lastly, only a prisoner who'd escaped, or was just released, would not mind where he was going."

The prisoner looked astonished. "To tell you the truth – " but Maude interrupted him.

"It would be much more convenient for us *not* to know the truth," she said, "but I am assuming you would not welcome the sight of a police-man."

"That is very true madame. And now if I may I have a question for you. You are a Catholic prison chaplain?"

"*Non*," said Maude briskly, "we are both Quaker prison ministers."

"Quakers – *qu'est-ce que c'est que ça*? I do not know what is that, Quakers?"

"Go on Dorothy, you explain. I'm driving. To Lille."

Dorothy took another deep breath, but then decided she would speak in exactly the same way she would to any prisoner coming to her in the prison for the first time.

"Quakers believe in the inner light and that of God in everyone. We believe we carry the truth within ourselves and we meet together in silence to worship and share. We have no priests, hymns, sermons or creeds."

"*Formidable*," said the Frenchman. "So you have no creeds and doctrines, but you do believe in God."

"I do," says Dorothy.

"Dorothy *thinks* she does, but I don't think she really does. Ask her what God is and she won't be able to explain. *I* don't believe in God."

"Although," Dorothy chimed in, "I think Maude does in fact believe in God, but just won't stick a label on something we know deep inside but don't understand."

"Wait a minute," said the Frenchman, speaking slowly. "Let me see if I have got this right. You are both Quakers, but madame Dorothy here believes in God but madame Maude thinks she does not, while madame Maude does not believe in God but madame Dorothy thinks she does."

"I think he's got it in one," observed Maude to her companion.

"*Extraordinaire*," said the Frenchman. "I think that you and I have much in common. You too are not heading for any port, so all winds must be the right ones for you too."

"If by that you mean we try to find the sacred in every moment, then I suppose that is true," said Dorothy.

It was in the midst of a detailed explanation by Maude of the Quaker business method that Dorothy remarked they had just driven through a red light.

"Pesky little things, they're set so low on those short posts in this country or else they're strung up high. And they're covered in dust. I don't know how you're meant to see them."

"Oh, Maude, look there's a policeman on a motorcycle beside me, I think he wants you to pull over."

Maude stopped the car and got out. She did not think that the gendarme would find her explanation for having failed to obey the red light convincing, and she was right. On top of that, he asked her whether she was aware that she had been speeding.

"Speeding?" she said indignantly. "Speeding? I was only doing 40 when the sign said 50."

"Kilometres per hour, madame, not miles," said the policeman, who had a large moustache and a commanding presence. Making it clear that any further discussion would be in vain, he slowly continued adding details to his blue notebook.

It was at this point that the Frenchman sprang out of the back of the

car. The ladies were visitors in their country. No harm had been done. The offences were minor. Their two countries had fought together in the war.

The prisoner's arms flapped wildly. He and the gendarme spoke on top of one another. The more excited the prisoner became, the more majestic and imperturbable the policeman became.

At length he snapped his notebook to. Putting it away in the midst of the gesticulating arms, he announced with great dignity, "*Bon*, I have noted down all the details in my *carnet*, madame. Your name, your address in England, the number of the vehicle. I shall be drawing up my report" – tapping his breast pocket solemnly – "tomorrow. Madame may either pay the fine at the town hall in Lille within the next seven days or the ticket will be sent to you in England. And unless you, monsieur, wish to be fined as well for obstructing law and order, I suggest you return to the car at once."

"It really was very brave of you to tackle the gendarme like that," said Dorothy as they drove out of the town. "I am just so glad that he didn't ask you any further questions."

"Thank you, madame Dorothy, I am glad too. But I have changed my mind about going to Lille, and would be obliged if you would drop me at the next town."

They did so. Maude and Dorothy got out of the car to say goodbye. "We are so grateful to you for taking our side with the policeman," said Maude. "It does all seem rather unfair. Still, I suppose we'll just have to face up to paying the fine. I expect God just wasn't watching over us," she said, shooting a pointed look at Dorothy.

"Mesdames, I am most grateful to you for your kindness, but do not worry about where God was or about the fine. It will never reach you."

"But he has my name and address and all the details."

"And I," said the prisoner, tapping his breast pocket, "I have his *carnet*."

# The Outsider

It was huge, it was black, it was menacing. As it emerged from the narrows into the more open water, the submarine appeared all at once to take up the entire loch. Its stub-nosed bow pushed a wall of water before it, silently, giving no quarter. It was an intruder, an alien that had no place amidst the beauty of the loch. Here, in just one boat, human ingenuity had assembled enough power to destroy the world.

As the monster bore down on Helen in her flimsy kayak, it seemed to hold her in its spell. Just moments before, the sunlight had been dancing on the water and, for all the tension of the occasion, Helen was aware of the splendour of the loch in its autumnal greens, golds and reds. In the distance, snow was already on the Scottish mountains. Now, a mountain of black was advancing upon her.

Quite how she had avoided the cordon of police boats she was not aware. All she knew was that, all of a sudden, she found herself alone on the still waters of the loch. Where had the other canoes and kayaks gone? Like all the others, she had ventured out onto the loch to protest against the coming of the first nuclear-armed Trident submarine to make its way to the base at Faslane on the Clyde. She had felt eager and excited: she was doing something, and something she believed in. She and many others had been doing all they could for fourteen years to prevent this very moment. But now, suddenly, she was scared. The great dark hulk loomed up much more quickly than she had expected. There was no escape. However fast she paddled – and her arms seemed frozen to her sides – she would not be able to escape the bow wave or the suction of the giant propellers.

Then, seemingly out of nowhere, an inflatable police dinghy roared up. One of the two policemen on board grabbed the end of Helen's kayak and, as the engine set up a great howl, she was dragged out of the submarine's path. Helen felt relieved – but also cheated. As they moved clear she shouted above the roar of the engine, "Have you come to arrest me?"

"No, we've come to save your life!" came the reply.

The massive shadow slipped by. Only then did she notice that uniformed sailors were standing on the lofty conning tower, from which festive flags were fluttering. She did not so much hear as feel the throbbing of the engines.

The rubber dinghy and kayak bobbed up and down in the wake of the massive vessel, and were also caught in the downdraught of a hovering helicopter.

"You're one very lucky and very stupid young woman!" shouted one of the policemen over the sound of the helicopter. "We're not arresting you but this is an official warning that we don't want to see you out here again."

On the verge of tears, Helen manoeuvred her kayak back through the choppy waters towards the shallows. The thin skin of her tiny craft grated on the gravel of the shore. A knot of waiting people cheered. Helen climbed out but her legs were trembling so much that she could barely stand. She fell into the arms of her friends. People on the bank began to sing "We shall overcome", but she was unable to join in. Someone brought her a cup of tea and wrapped a blanket round her shoulders as she sat shivering on a rock.

What had the point of her gesture been? She felt like a drop of water shaken off a dog's coat. Her action had not stopped the submarine. She had not changed anybody's mind. Had she, as the Quakers were fond of saying, spoken truth to power? Or had she just risked her own life and even that of the two policemen for no real purpose? She was tired, she

was afraid, she was confused – and yet she felt borne along by a great host of friends, both seen and unseen. Maybe this was the way the world changed. Maybe it was in our helplessness and weakness, in the togetherness – but the words would not come.

She needed to be alone. As darkness fell and everyone drifted away, Helen stayed on by herself beside the loch. Her friends were worried about her, but she insisted that she would be all right. They loaded the kayak up on the roof of her car and she agreed to join them later at the youth hostel.

Lights on the far shore began to be reflected on the silky black waters of the loch. By the water's edge Helen noticed a duck and a drake paddling in the shallows. She half expected to see a line of ducklings, but of course it was too late in the year for that.

The ducks reminded her of a story a Canadian Quaker had told her. One day she was by the lakeside where she lived, watching a duck and her eleven ducklings paddling about.

"All at once," she said, "the mother duck set up an constant, urgent chatter. Looking up, I saw the dark shape of an intruder: a bald eagle, circling overhead.

"The eagle descended like a jumbo jet, its huge wings spread out and talons stretched out before of it. Just as it reached the little group, the mother duck said 'Now!!' and the whole lot dived as one. The eagle's talons raked the water, but came up with nothing.

"The duck and eleven ducklings resurfaced. The eagle circled again. The mother duck kept up her urgent chatter and, as the jumbo jet came in again, gave the command. Twelve tails went up into the air and disappeared into the water. Once again the vicious talons scythed through the water but without result.

"Eight times the great bird circled; eight times the duck chattered constantly to her brood; eight times she gave the command to dive, and eight times the eagle failed to make a strike. After the eighth attempt, it gave up and flew away."

How, Helen wondered, had the duck been able to communicate so precisely with her offspring, and how did those fluffballs know so exactly what to do? They too were weak; they too were up against a mighty intruder; and by sticking together and acting as one they survived.

Somewhere, in the cave of memory, the story reminded Helen of something that had happened before. She got up, went to the car and drove the few miles to the Faslane base. Near the South gate she parked the car at the peace camp.

She set out on foot towards the North gate, over a mile away. After ten minutes or so, Helen stopped. The fence all looked the same but she was sure that this was the spot. It was here that eight years before, in the spring, she and some others had cut their way through the chain-link fence. It had not been difficult to get in. It was the 4th of April 1984 and the anniversary of the death sixteen years before of Martin Luther King, who had done so much to promote the rights of black people in America.

They had illegally, but not violently, entered the grounds of the base. Once inside, they began digging. Sure enough, the police with their dogs arrived before long. They were arrested without offering any resistance, but she smiled as she recalled the look of astonishment on the face of the Inspector when he had demanded to know what they were doing.

"Planting potatoes," they replied.

"Planting potatoes?" said the Inspector blankly.

"Planting potatoes," they confirmed.

The Inspector, who had been hiding behind all sorts of official police language ("I am arresting you for unauthorised entry of protected land," "anything you say may be taken down and..."), dropped his mask.

"Potatoes – what on earth are you planting potatoes for?"

"Because we want the soil to be restored to its proper use. We want things to grow in this beautiful area that has now been given over to death. It is the most peaceful thing we could think of doing."

Ten months later Helen was sent to prison. In court, she said that for her, the base at Faslane was morally wrong. It could never be right to use these ghastly weapons. The world was God's creation. Out of love for her adopted Vietnamese goddaughter and out of love for the world, she had had to act. She could not keep silent. A gospel of love could not be defended by threatening to kill millions of innocent people.

She was fined a small sum – £30 – but refused to pay and was sentenced to five days in prison.

Five days for planting potatoes. It was not a long time, and yet it was as though a whole lifetime had been crammed into those few days. She remembered vividly how the first electronically operated steel door had swung back. Just five days ... but what lay ahead? There could be some hardened and perhaps violent offenders inside, who might not take kindly to the fact that she had gone to an ultra-respectable all-girls school. What would they make of the fact that she had been arrested for breaking into a military base? It was all very well making fine-sounding statements in court, but this was a moment of truth.

She had to strip. She had to take a freezing cold shower. She had to put on stiff, rough prison clothes that didn't fit properly. Her clumpy shoes came with three pairs of laces, but when she gave away one pair of laces to a woman who had none at all she was shouted at. "It's against the rules to give something away!"

It was cold and they had forgotten to give her a cardigan. So she put on her anorak. She was shouted at again. "It's against the rules! Anoraks are to be worn outside only!"

It was a grey place: grey because the windows were small and dirty, grey because it was a place of shadows, real and imagined, grey because it was a world of harshness, sadness and struggle. The other women carried a lifetime of greyness in every line on their faces. Some were defiant, others cowed.

The woman in the next-door cell who was admitted at the same time as Helen spent the first night shivering with cold. "Hasn't your cell got a heater? Why didn't you switch it on?"

"I didn't know you were allowed," said the woman nervously. "Don't you need permission?"

That was at breakfast. When Helen asked if she could have vegetarian food, she was marched back to her cell. "Prisoners on special diet eat in their own cells!" she was told, as the door slammed to. She felt helpless, confused and angry. A notice was pinned to the door saying, "All meals must be eaten on her own!" But then she remembered another rule they had been told about, that hunger strikers had to sit with the others. So she stuffed her meal into the bin, told the warders she wasn't eating and at lunch was back with the others. Now it was the warders who were confused and angry.

Word had got round that Helen was inside for refusing to pay a £30 fine. The women clustered around her curiously wanting to know why. "Couldn't you afford it, hen?"

Before Helen could reply, one of the other women had said, "She's against the bomb."

"Oh, you're against nuclear weapons!" said one of the toughest looking women, giving her a hug. "You did this for us! You did this for all our children!"

The strange thing, looking back, Helen thought, was that the world inside prison and the people in it had somehow seemed more real than the outside world. In the prison, despite all the differences between them, in many ways she felt as close to the other women as it was possible to be. In the "real" world people fought wars and let children starve. They were cruel to animals. They cut down trees that had stood for hundreds of years to turn them into chipboard. There, in prison, there had been nowhere to hide. It was the way it would be eight years later, all alone on the loch, feeling helpless, exposed and afraid – and yet connected.

Just as she had felt so supported when most alone on the water, so also she remembered sitting on her bunk in the cell surrounded by cards and letters from friends and well-wishers. It was in surrender, it was when one was broken, that true change could happen. Was this how God worked? Was this what God meant, or even what God was? What mattered was not the helplessness and sense of futility but the strength of discovering that one was deeply connected, in the same way that the prisoners had embraced the outsider in their midst, and the ducklings, acting as one, had survived the powerful intruder.

# Silent Friendship

John sat up straight in bed. It was the middle of the night. He felt confused. There he had been, minding his own business and having a good sleep, when a poem came to him. It came to him so strongly that it woke him up.

He switched on the light. Scrabbling about he found a pencil and bit of paper and jotted the poem down. He switched off the light again and went back to sleep.

In the morning, as he got up, he came across the scrap of paper. He had almost forgotten about the poem.

He looked at it in surprise. It rhymed and it had a catchy rhythm. Not like modern poems, he thought, where anything goes, but a good old-fashioned poem. A bit childish, perhaps, at first reading, but it also made you think. Whoever the author was obviously liked to play with words. Part of it went:

> When that of God in me is you
> And that of God in All is One
> Then all Man's Sight sees with One Light
> As bright and timeless as the Sun.

John put the event down as a surprising and rather delightful experience. Perhaps it had come from the heavy gardening he was doing the day before?

Three nights later another poem came. Once more it was such a ready-formed poem that he felt the least he could do was switch on the light and write it down. There it was the next morning, like something that had dropped out of the sky.

A few nights later two poems came. Sometimes as many as three and on one occasion even five poems came through. Writing them down in the middle of the night became a bit of a chore. So John bought a hand-held dictating machine, which he kept under his pillow. It was about the size of a mobile phone. All he had to do was press a button, speak in the poem, and go back to sleep.

Often, in the morning, he would totally have forgotten the poem. It would be like a dream that had slipped out of mind altogether or which one couldn't remember properly. But here was the evidence. All he had to do was write the poem up and pop in some punctuation.

They began to come during the day as well. Once he was in a supermarket. On the back of his shopping list he scribbled:

wHoly Be and you will see
You ARE your whole True Self!
Your other I can quietly die
Or rest upon the shelf.

Now can you be the Love that burns
In every human heart,
The Light that springs from everything;
You are ALL – and yet take part.

Who were these poems for, he asked himself? For everyone, or just for him? When after a number of years the flow didn't stop, and he had received nearly 6,000 poems, he said to himself sternly that the time had come for A Silent Testimony. A poem emerged in the night called "A Word in Thine Ear".

Our Non-Proliferation Treaty,
  Lord, I hereby state
I really must decline to sign,
  For YOU proliferate!

I am averse to writing verse,
  But You refuse to hear
And as before send more and more
  Than I'm prepared to bear.

That's telling him, he thought – except that it was really God telling God through him that it was all too much for him and that all he wanted was silence. It made his head spin.

He decided to call on his friend Len. Len was 92. Like John, Len wrote to a prisoner on death row in America. John had been writing to someone for a few years and suggested to Len that he might like to too. Len wrote to a man called Warren, in Arizona.

Len lived by himself in a little cottage near the sea. "Come in!" his voice rang out when John knocked on the door.

John went into the snug sitting room. "I'm glad you've come, John, " said Len. "I have a problem. It's to do with Warren. Read this."

He handed John a letter. John could see from the American stamps and the familiar yellow paper that it was from a prisoner, but it was not from Warren.

"Let me introduce myself," the letter began. "I'm Bill. For several years now I have been Warren's neighbour. The thing is, he can't read or write. Every time he gets a letter from you he passes it through the bars to me and I read it out to him. He then dictates a reply. So the words are his, but he has been kinda afraid to tell you he can't write in case you didn't like the idea and stopped writing.

"Trouble is, I've been moved to a different cell and his new neighbour is not what you might say the helpful type. The only way you could keep the correspondence going would be for you to send Warren tapes. He has an audio cassette so it should work okay."

John looked up at Len. "So what's the problem with sending him tapes?"

"I don't have a tape recorder," said Len. "Anyway, my eyesight's going and I've been thinking that it's time for me to give up the writing. I can hardly see to put the address on the envelope and can't get down the street to the post box like I used to."

"Problem solved," said John. "In fact it all works out quite neatly. You want to stop writing and Warren can't read. I have a tape recorder I never use so you can borrow that and I'm happy to drop in and parcel up and post the tapes."

Which is what they did for several years. Len loved receiving the tapes and also enjoyed dictating his thoughts. He soon discovered that it was a whole lot easier to speak for an hour or so than to write! Besides, he was now totally blind and it was the only way in which he could communicate.

Len told Warren how he had been a builder and liked using his hands. Warren sent a tape saying that he too liked using his hands. He was good at drawing, as Len knew from the sketches he sent, and he also liked carving animals from wood, but the prison authorities would not let him have carving tools.

Len would also tell Warren about his Quaker friend John and the poems that came to him so strangely in the night. "I'd like to share one particular one he wrote for his own penfriend," he said. "When he read it out to me it said exactly what I feel about you and me. In fact, I won't read it out myself but I will get John to speak it into the machine when next he's here. I'll just have to make sure I leave enough space at the end of the tape. That'll make me shut up and stop being such a wind-bag!"

At the end of the tape came John's voice:

No Limits

Friend, though the prison shuts you in,
  So also does your bag of skin;
So don't forget! Your Spirit-mind
  Can never, never be confined.

The Love in you, the Love in me
  Can timelessly cross every sea,
Lead through windows, dance through doors –
  For your Love's mine and my Love yours.

You may be black and I be white,
  Yet both of us are still One Light,
Share one air and share one Sun –
  All of us are wHoly One.

One day, John went round to pick up a tape from Len to post. Len was upset. He had received another letter from Bill, Warren's former neighbour. It said that Warren's ancient tape recorder had finally died. Under the prison regulations prisoners were allowed to keep old tape recorders but were not allowed to buy new ones. So Warren would not be able to communicate any more.

No more padded bags with tapes arrived. "I know you like a silence,

John, what with being bombarded with all those poems, but I do miss hearing from Warren and worry that he's all right," Len said sadly.

Then, a few weeks later, a small box arrived from Arizona. It contained a tiny three-masted boat carved out of a cake of soap. Len cradled it in his giant builder's hand, going over and over it with his fingers until he could almost "see" the boat. He held it out to John.

"What do you think of it?" he asked.

"Why," said John, "it's beautiful. I just wish you could see it for yourself."

"I don't need to, my friend. It says everything that there is to be said. But how do I thank Warren? Perhaps you or your friend up there could write a poem about it!"

"I can already think of a title," said John wonderingly. "I would call the poem "Silent Friend-Ship.""

# The Opinion Poll

"Just as a matter of interest," said the editor of the local *Herald*, leaning back in his leather swivel chair, "what do you two know about Quakers?"

"Quakers?" asked Andrew. "Not much."

"Me neither," said Sally.

"Well, it says here that in a recent survey just 1% of people in Oxford Street had ever heard of Quakers, while just 20% of the general public know anything about them at all. Come on, you're two bright junior reporters, what would you say you know about them?"

"They're something to do with porridge oats and wear funny black hats, like on the cereal packets. I think they're some kind of religious sect – I know, Puritans, that's what they are," said Sally brightly.

"Andrew?"

"Um, I don't know much more really. I'd say they live in America but have died out in this country. Are they the ones who live in farming communities and don't have electricity?"

"No, that's the Amish, Andrew," said Sally. "I think – they're against violence and war. And they're vegetarians and don't drink alcohol."

"Anything else?"

The two bright junior reporters were silent.

The editor, William Hamilton, leaned back even further in his swivel chair. "I can't say I know much about them myself, but if the public is so ignorant – and you two sound like a pretty good sample – I think we should run an article on them. It's Friday now, but do something for next week. Read up about them, ask people in the street what they know about them and even interview a real live Quaker, if you can find one round here."

"That would be scary," said Sally. "But – can we start with you as a member of the public and ask what *you* know about Quakers? Didn't you do a history degree?"

"It was history of art," said the editor hastily. "But okay, give me a few minutes and I'll jot down what I think I know."

When Sally and Andrew returned ten minutes later the editor handed them an envelope with jotted down on the back:

*English religious sect, founded by James Fox. Went to America with Pilgrim Fathers. Conscientious objectors and pacifists. Narrow-minded and strict. Say thee and thou. Regard taking oaths as swearing. Have female priests (Elizabeth Fry) and make chocolate (Cadbury's). Men wear beards and sandals.*

"That's pretty impressive," said Andrew. "Where did you learn all that, Mr Hamilton?"

"Oh, one picks these things up," said the editor breezily. "And once again, William's the name – no need for all that mister stuff! It's all first names these days, and much better too, if you ask me. But I bet the Quakers don't use first names!"

* * *

"It says here," said Andrew peering at his monitor, "that they're really called the Religious Society of Friends. Their churches are called meeting houses and their services meetings for worship."

"And I've discovered," said Sally, "that there is a Quaker meeting right here! Why don't we go along on Sunday as part of our research?"

"I couldn't bear it," said Andrew. "I loathe organised religion."

"Come on, this is in the line of duty," said Sally. "It would be just one hour out of your life. Anyway, what is it that you dislike so much about organised religion?"

"Well, I could do without priests, dogma, hymns, sermons, prayers, and Bible readings for a start."

"Oh," said Sally, "doesn't leave much, does it? What would you do – just sit there in silence?"

"No, I guess I'd want some meditation and then to share some really deep thoughts from time to time. Well, and perhaps I would have some readings, but not just from the Bible but from other great Scriptures as well. What about you? What would you want in a religion?"

Sally was silent and thought for a moment. "I'd want something that made me feel connected with everyone and the world. Something that was simple and yet had mystery – oh, and where women were equal with men."

"There's no such thing, I'm afraid," said Andrew. "Anyway, let's see what else this website has to say about Quakers."

"No!" exclaimed Sally. "No more reading. Let's just go along with a totally open mind."

"Okay," said Andrew. "I'll get on with that other story about the helium balloon that drifted all the way from France and landed in the park. I'm hoping Mr – I mean William – might let me fly to Paris to meet that kid whose name and address were on the label."

"Flying's bad for the environment, Andrew," observed Sally sternly.

\* \* \*

It was Sunday morning. Andrew straightened his tie. He hated wearing a jacket and tie. But as Sally said, it was all in the line of duty. And maybe she'd think he looked quite smart, too. They hadn't been with the newspaper for long and he had been wanting to ask her out. Perhaps they could combine business with pleasure. But it would be kind of weird for their first date to be a Quaker meeting.

They met up at the station. From there it was a short walk up the hill to the Meeting House. Sally was smartly dressed as well.

"I think it must be just up here," said Andrew, looking at the map he had printed off the internet. "That white building on the other side of the road."

"Can't be," said Sally. "There are all sorts of scruffy people in jeans going inside. Probably a jumble sale or something."

But it was the Quaker meeting house. At the door they were welcomed with a warm smile by an elderly woman.

"Hello, dears, I'm Pat. Is this your first time at a Quaker meeting?"

"It is," said Sally.

"Well, perhaps you'd like to take this little leaflet in with you. It tells you a bit about what to expect. But it's all very simple, really."

Seeing the puzzled looks on their faces, she went on, "Just go in through the door there and sit wherever you like. People sit in silence, that's all. It's a bit like a meditation. Sometimes someone might say a few words if they feel so moved."

"What about the priest?" asked Andrew.

"We don't have priests."

"Oh. What about hymns?"

"We don't sing hymns."

"Blimey," he said softly, hoping the woman hadn't heard.

They went over to the meeting room, where a man wearing neither sandals nor a beard opened the door for them. He smiled too.

They went in. Apart from a few children they were greeted by what was largely a sea of grey hair. The chairs were arranged in circles. They tucked themselves away at the back.

Having stared at the carpet for several minutes, Andrew looked up cautiously expecting that everyone would be staring at them. Instead they were nearly all simply sitting there quietly with their eyes closed. No-one was taking any notice of them at all – except that, in a strange way, it felt as though they *were* all taking notice, not of him and Sally but of everything around them. He couldn't quite put his finger on it, but it was as though he was being swept up in the quiet feeling in the room.

Sally, meanwhile, had looked all round the room, noticed the simple little arrangement of yellow tulips and bright blue forget-me-nots on the table (mother always says that forget-me-nots are weeds, she thought to herself), and had taken a good if discreet look at all the people there. The room was plain and simple. The chairs, she noticed, were blue plastic.

The easiest thing seemed to be to close one's eyes. Andrew, it seemed, had done the same. She too was just beginning to feel strangely peaceful when, for no apparent reason, several adults and all the children got up and quietly left the room. Oh, that must be the children's class, she realised.

After about twenty minutes an elderly woman got to her feet. She explained how difficult it was for her to be losing her hearing but that in some ways it was a blessing. It got rid of distractions and made it easier to listen to the "still small voice within". Sometimes, in life, we had to give things up to find what had been there all along.

A few minutes later a man got up and spoke about living life simply. He mentioned an American Quaker in the eighteenth century called John Woolman who was a tailor and a farmer. He wore undyed woollen clothes and spoke of getting rid of "cumber" in one's life. People thought that he might be a little bit mad, but they came to realise how deep his principles were and that he was living out what he believed.

Some time later a woman got up and said that of the four great Quaker testimonies to peace, truth, equality and simplicity, she thought the one to simplicity was the most beautiful. "Get simplicity right," she said, "and peace, truth and equality follow naturally."

She sat down again. Right towards the end of the meeting, a man got up and said that he had never thought of it before, but you could take any one of peace, truth, equality and simplicity and, if it were lived out, it would lead to the others. "Perhaps there is just one great testimony."

A few minutes later two people shook hands, and soon everyone else in the room was shaking their neighbours' hands as well.

Afterwards, during notices, they were invited to introduce themselves. Andrew mentioned his name and that this was his first meeting, and mumbled something about how it had been very different from what he had expected. Sally added that they were both from the local newspaper and had been asked to do an article on Quakerism. "We look forward to that. We could do with knowing what we're all about!" said the woman giving out notices. People laughed.

Over tea and coffee people came up and asked if they lived locally and how long they'd worked for the paper. Oddly enough, no-one seemed particularly anxious to explain what Quakerism was about. They were given some books and leaflets.

At length, as people began to drift away, Sally and Andrew were left talking to the doorkeeper and the woman who had given out the notices. "I'm sorry that people bombarded you with literature like that," the woman said. "You must think that we are all trying to convert you, when in fact we are not, as there is nothing to convert you to."

"Oh, Rachel, of course there is," said the man. "It's just that Quakerism's something people have to discover for themselves."

"It's all right," said Sally, "no-one has been pressuring us. We just wanted to find out what Quakers believe."

"We all believe something different," said the woman firmly. "You have to find your own truth."

"But it's more than that," protested her companion gently, "or we could all just stay at home and meditate on our own. That's why we meet in silence, waiting on the Spirit."

"Is the Spirit the same as God?" asked Andrew.

"It is to me, but others prefer not to use the word God," he replied.

"I'm puzzled," said Andrew. "Does that mean that Quakers do or don't believe in God?"

"Yes," and "No," came the answer at the same time.

*   *   *

It was then, Sally and Andrew explained a year later when they got married in the meeting house, that they knew they were in the right place.

# Drawing the Threads Together

The last stitch had been put into place and drawn tight. It was done. Seven years work, and now it was complete. Margaretta felt a great sense of accomplishment, as well as an unexpected sense of emptiness. There it was, the long tapestry panel capturing scenes from her family's life, on which she had worked so lovingly and patiently for so long. She knew, looking at it, that it was this more than anything that she would want to rescue from the house if there were a fire.

Her 10-year-old granddaughter Rachel came into the room. The panel was almost as tall as she was.

"It's beautiful, Grandmother. I love all the scenes. What are you going to do now that it's finished, Grandmother?" she asked.

"Now that's just what I have been asking myself, Rachel," said Margaretta. "Do you know, I feel a bit lost now that it is done."

The two of them pored over every scene depicted on the panel. Rachel knew every one of them well, as the panel had been a part of her life for as long as she could remember, and she loved to see the way it had grown each time she visited, how each scene built up, stitch by stitch. But she wanted to hear her grandmother tell every detail of every story again. It brought her family to life.

"Oh look," she said, "here's the one showing me and the family going to Canada to join Dad out there! And Auntie Anthea getting married and Grandfather retiring as a doctor; and here's Uncle Quentin, making his beautiful violins; what made him choose that as his job, Grandmother?"

Margaretta willingly answered all Rachel's questions, but the hardest one was, "Will you be doing another family tapestry, Grandmother? Please say you will!"

Her grandmother had in fact already been wondering whether to embark on another tapestry, but somehow it didn't feel right to do anything after completing something so dear to her heart. So each time she felt the urge to add a few stitches, she would read a book or do some gardening.

Then, not longer after, sitting in the garden, she read a short letter in the Quaker magazine *The Friend*. It suggested the idea of telling the story of Quakerism in the form of individual tapestry panels. Margaretta felt as though the letter was meant for her. She dashed off a reply.

Later, she found out that hers was the first letter that Anne had received. They discovered that they were both members of the Royal Academy in London, where they arranged to meet in a special members' room. Everyone else was very prim and proper, but Anne and Margaretta were in a state of high excitement and there were many astonished glances as Anne demonstrated to Margaretta the stitch she had invented specially for the purpose.

"It's really two stitches, you see. You start with an ordinary stem stitch, like this," she said, holding up the tapestry backing, while the other silent members secretly peered at them over their newspapers, "and then you do a split stitch."

"A split stitch?"

"Yes, a split stitch. The wool we will be using is made of two strands and as your needle comes up out of the backing you pass it through the two strands of the last stitch. That makes for a really firm stitch and is excellent when it comes to lettering — and there will be lots of lettering, as we need to explain the pictures we will be embroidering."

Margaretta had already sent a sample piece of embroidery to Anne. It showed two soldiers forming part of a tapestry of Derby Gaol, which Anne was planning. The soldiers were guarding George Fox after he had been thrown into prison.

Anne smiled. "You've done red jackets, Margaretta – but they should have been blue in 1650! However, what I would really like you to do is a panel of Swarthmoor Hall."

"Oh yes," said Margaretta, "that's where Quakerism really began! It's the house where George Fox lived later on, after he married Margaret Fell. I'd love to do that."

It was quite a difficult panel, showing the Fell family, together with servants, sitting around a fire in the Great Hall and a weary George Fox returning on an even wearier horse. At the bottom was the inscription, "A matter of sixty ministers did the Lord raise up and send abroad out of the north country." These were the "valiant sixty", who were to travel to the south of England, continental Europe and America with the Quaker message, just as all the panels were to tell the story of Quakerism.

Margaretta tried to excite others with the idea but, apart from some of the children, Friends were strangely uninterested. "A waste of Quaker money," they would say. So she did the panel all by herself.

At the same time, there was a strong sense of rightness about the venture. The right people were coming forward at the right time, almost without being asked. There was an energy in the air, as though what they were doing was meant to be, guided by an unseen hand.

\* \* \*

And that was also how it began. Anne was taking the children's class, in Taunton. All they had was a small and shabby side-room. It needed cheering up. The only child in the class one Sunday was a 12-year-old boy, Jonathan.

Anne suggested that they might do some coloured pictures to brighten up the room. Jonathan was tired of doing coloured pictures in the children's class. He suggested something more adventurous. Remembering that Anne liked needlework, he said, "Couldn't we sew it, or something like that? What about a collage, or mosaic?"

The idea would not leave her. One winter's morning, in January 1981, Anne was doing the washing-up. She stood there, half in a dream, looking without really seeing the bubbles and the patterns on the breakfast dishes. All at once it was there, inside her head, a picture of how it might be – no, of how it *would* be, the story of Quakerism in stitching. The Quaker Tapestry was born.

\* \* \*

These thoughts were going through Margaretta's head as she finished the panel on Swarthmoor Hall.

My dearest Rachel,
    You will remember how flat I felt when the family panel was finished. Well, now I have finished a Quaker panel. It shows Swarthmoor Hall, where Judge Fell allowed his wife Margaret

and George Fox and other early Quakers to hold meetings for worship. That was dangerous, as it was not permitted, but as Thomas Fell was a judge no one dared confront him. I did it all by myself, but now I have another challenge which is to do a panel on conscientious objection. Do you know what that is? Conscientious objectors were the people who refused to serve in the First World War, as they did not believe in fighting and killing other people. There will be a picture of a young man before a tribunal, with neatly dressed women holding out white feathers as a symbol of cowardice. How unjust that was! We will also be showing them working as hospital orderlies or agricultural workers instead. I say "we", because I am going to be helped by the children from my meeting! I have already taught them the special Quaker stitch we use, showing them how to roll the needle between finger and thumb to form a cord. They are so quick and love it!

And later she wrote:

We had a special tea party with the children where each of them added a gold leaf to the bare tree in the panel. They did the drawing for the tree, as well as drawings of the hospital orderly I told you about, scrubbing the floor, and the agricultural worker, behind the plough. The plough was drawn by a big, powerful draught horse. The children knew that this kind of horse – a Suffolk Punch – had short, clean legs but when the picture came back for the tapestry, frilly bits had been added. We decided that this might explain why the horse looks so astonished and wide-eyed!

By the time the third of Margaretta's panels, on True Health, was done some years later, all sorts of "tapestresses", as her husband Sacha called the band of people who showed up at his house, were now keen to help. It was another complicated tapestry, with many scenes. It showed a horse-drawn bathing machine, Joseph Lister of antiseptics fame, and Dr Alfred Salter and his wife Ada, who did so much to help the poor and improve public health in parts of London around 1900.

Margaretta shared the work out among Friends all over East Anglia. Once she took the partly finished panel by train from Cambridge to

Peterborough, handed it over on the platform to Marjorie, who was responsible for the next part of the work, and dashed across the platform to catch the next train back to Cambridge.

One of the last things Margaretta and her team completed in the panel was a bed with a whole family in it, designed to show the terrible overcrowding that was once so common.

"What are these things we are meant to be embroidering beneath the bed, Margaretta?" asked one of her group.

"They're rats," replied Margaretta. "It's meant to show how over-crowding brought disease."

"Well, I just can't make them look like rats. They look more like tiny ducks, or butterflies, but definitely not rats."

Margaretta tried her hand at the rats. They all practised pointy tails and little black snouts.

"It gets worse and worse," said Margaretta. "They just look like little racing cars. I think the only thing to do is to turn them into beetles!"

*I've finished my third and last panel,* Margaretta wrote to Rachel. *So many other people were working on other panels, in England and all over the world, that there is nothing further for us to do.*

Once again, Margaretta had the familiar feeling of being at a loss. Rachel and her family came over from Canada again. She showed Rachel, now a young woman, photographs of all the panels that had been made.

"What a story you've all told!" exclaimed Rachel. "Just like you cap-tured the history of our family in your panel, now you've told the story of Quakerism. Each panel conveys a little bit."

"Yes, that's right," said Margaretta. "It's so hard to pin down exactly what Quakerism is. It's like a jewel, with many facets. It's only by look-ing at a number of them that you get an idea of what it's all about. It's what people do, not what they believe, that matters – the people who helped abolish slavery, who made prisons better places, or who were prepared to go to prison themselves rather than fight. It's what we call testimony."

"Is that the same as ministry, Grandmother?"

"No, that's when people get up to speak in meeting for worship. It can be about testimony, and is like a tapestry too, except that people weave with words. They can even weave with silence; just sitting quietly in meeting is a form of ministry."

"I don't understand."

"Well, you see, everyone there is drawn together like the threads in a tapestry. You need some who are bright, and others who are more subdued. You need some in the foreground and some in the background. You need some who go out and do things, and others who lead quiet lives. Everyone in a meeting plays their part. When you feel the quaking and get to your feet, you often find afterwards that what you were saying was what those who were silent were thinking."

"Have you often spoken in meeting, Grandmother?"

Margaretta thought for a moment. "When I first came to Quakerism, it was in a small meeting, just ten or so people. That was in Whitby, in Yorkshire. I was not much older than you. As the meetings were so small, almost everyone would minister from time to time; otherwise the meetings would mostly have been all silent. But then we moved to Cambridge, where there was a big meeting. It wasn't quite so easy there."

"Why was that, Grandmother?"

"Well, there were a lot of clever people there and many who had been Quakers all their lives, unlike me. Many of the women were still dressed in black. It's over forty years ago now, but I still remember one occasion as though it were yesterday. My heart was thumping, and I just had to get to my feet and speak. I don't have a loud voice, as you know, and besides I'd been used to our meetings in Whitby with a few Friends in a small room. After just a few sentences a female voice behind me rang out sternly, 'Our Friend is not heard!'

"I stammered a few more words and sat down. No doubt that was how Quakers asked someone to speak up, but I did wonder whether there could not have been some kinder way of doing things. I didn't minister much again after that."

"But Grandmother, look at the panels! Your ministry has been to draw the threads together. The panels have been – and always will be! – *your* ministry."

Lightning Source UK Ltd.
Milton Keynes UK
UKOW02f112281016
286316UK00002B/169/P

9 780955 618314